The White Horse

By

Rebecca Harrison

For Adam and Dad

Praise for
The White Horse

"An evocative lyrical gothic tale with twists, secrets, and poetry. Charlotte, a composer whose world is musical, was a brave and entertaining heroine from page one to the final, tense chapter. A joy to read."

    Darcie Little Badger, Nebula Award-winning author of *Elatsoe* and *A Snake Falls to Earth*

"Harrison's haunting novella will sweep readers away to a terrifying place of folk tales and suspicion. She has masterfully crafted a Brontë-esque tale, entwined with horror and surreal, eerie descriptions, that kept me hooked until the very last sentence. I loved it."

    Katherine Livesey, author of the *Sisters of Shadow* trilogy

"Harrison's *The White Horse* is a stirring symphony of gothic fantasy and folk horror in harmony, told via an enchanting lead character whose musically-inclined way of viewing the world is something worth singing about."

    Patrick Barb, author of *Gargantuana's Ghost* and *Helicopter Parenting in the Age of Drone Warfare*

"A fascinating read reminiscent of the most poetic strains of Cormac McCarthy, and one that gets more fascinating with the turn of every page. At times there's an almost Tolkein-esque folksy quality to *The White Horse*, but this is expertly counterbalanced with a contemporary feel that will appeal to modern sensibilities."

    Gavin Gardiner, author of *For Rye*

Chapter One	1
Chapter Two	11
Chapter Three	21
Chapter Four	33
Chapter Five	43
Chapter Six	53
Chapter Seven	63
Chapter Eight	73
Chapter Nine	79
Chapter Ten	89
Chapter Eleven	99
Chapter Twelve	107
Chapter Thirteen	115
Chapter Fourteen	123
Chapter Fifteen	133
Chapter Sixteen	143
Chapter Seventeen	153
Chapter Eighteen	161
Chapter Nineteen	171
Chapter Twenty	181
Chapter Twenty-One	187
Epilogue	193

Chapter One

"Do you dare stand on the White Horse's eye and see what the White Horse sees?"

The sun is tucked in Pa Mountberry's face. Emmie pulls me around dried sheep muck. Her hand is sweaty. Our hems trip in cowslips and daisies, yet Ma Mountberry holds her skirts like the grass offends her.

"What does the White Horse see?" I ask. But Pa Mountberry doesn't hear me because the whole world is climbing with us all the way until we see right out to where the Earth curves. The land's just pieces and shapes now we're above it. I could put fields in my pocket. The wind is full of laughter: it whips us. Emmie squeezes my hand. She smells of the sugared almonds we sucked in our coach. Her dark hair blows in my face and tickles my nose.

"We're so high, we'll float off if we let go of each other," she says.

"You be my anchor and I'll be yours," I say, and I stomp heavy as I can. But folk are faster and jostle us along. I can't help but gawp at the country women with their scarlet capes all twisting and flinging. Blue butterflies catch in the capes and flit and dart their way out. I hold my breath until they're free.

"Will you race for the cheese, Papa?" Emmie points to the yeoman rolling a wheel of cheese.

"And break my back fifty times before I reach the valley?" He pauses and looks down the falling way, and I look too, so hard I think I see the bustard birds dancing — fan tails and squark. "I don't think so, Emmie, but your mother has said she intends to win the ladies pipe smoking contest."

"Will you, Mama?" Emmie asks. But Ma Mountberry swats the laugh away like flies and doesn't smile. There used to be pretty in her face, but now it's just in her portraits.

"I didn't know there were so many folk in the world," Emmie says.

"There were upwards of twenty-five thousand at the last Pastime, but I don't believe there's ever been a crowd such as this." Pa Mountberry says. The climb is in his voice. "Well, Emmie, how about you and Lottie count them all? After all, you girls don't want to see the fellows falling flat on their faces chasing the pig, or plummeting after the cheese, or the ladies puffing hoops of smoke from their pipes. And you certainly won't want any victuals or to have someone tell you your fortune." He laughs and it spins off in the winds. Emmie drops my hand and turns round and round, counting faster and faster before coming to a dizzy stop.

"I've counted them all, and it's all the folk in the world." She spreads her hands wide. Chatter booms over the sky. The day smells of chalk and ale and games. Shouts echo and bounce. Booths scatter the hilltop, wind-flapped, with queues and coin sounds and ginger smelling steam. My mouth waters.

"Emmie, let's get some gingerbread."

"May we, Papa?"

"Well…" Pa Mountberry scratches his chin. Emmie pouts until her face is a grizzly prune. He laughs and presses a coin in her palm. "That's your prize for winning the gurning contest." Sun flashes on the coin and pinches my eyes. Emmie closes her fist around it. Someone bumps my shoulder.

"Girls, don't stray too far," Ma Mountberry says. But her gaze is nettles on me, just like when she used to talk about sending me back where I came from. And I shiver even through the May heat, even through the sweltering crowd. I nearly shiver back to when I was little, when my Ma wouldn't wake no matter how I tugged her hand or put daisies in her hair. When Pa Mountberry was Lord Mountberry carrying me from that dark smell. When Emmie was Miss Emmeline with no willow brook in her voice, and I gave her the buttercup I clutched in the coach, for her skin was so pale, I thought she needed its shine on her.

"I'm trusting Lottie Lion to keep you safe from any dangers," Pa Mountberry says.

"Dangers?" Emmie rolls her eyes.

"See over there?" He points, but all I see is crowd, and I tilt my head to try to look through gaps, but there are none. "That's where Saint George slayed the dragon. No grass grows where the dragon's blood fell. And not far from where we stand, Alfred the Great defeated the Vikings."

"Emmie." I nudge her with my elbow, for Pa Mountberry is telling us Uffington history, and if we don't escape, we'll be listening to every bit of it, and there will be no warm gingerbread sticking to the roofs of our mouths. Drumming sounds blast over us. Someone yells about rope walkers.

"Aren't you going to join the sack race, Papa?" Emmie says. And as he pauses, she grabs my hand, and we duck into the crowd. Everything bustles about us until the world is a spinning of laughter and sky. Kestrels hover above booths, dive for drops of pickled walnuts and beef, then glide into the faraway. I scrunch my eyes until they disappear. "We should have our fortunes told," Emmie says.

"I'll tell you your fortune – we're going to live together until we've very old, older than these hills, and we'll supper on sugared almonds every day until all our teeth fall out," I say. More booths. I take great gulps of gingerbread smell. We join the queue behind a broad man in a smock. I count the folk in front of us. I'm itchy with waiting.

"Lottie, I dropped the penny," Emmie says. We both turn and look along the trampled way, where the grass bends into hems and donkey hooves and boots and boots and boots. There are too many folk with swift eyes and swifter hands. I bet some boy has it in his stinky palm. "We'll never find it, Lottie. We can't tell Mama. You know what she'll say." I don't need to nod. Ma Mountberry nips at me with her words and glares. She calls me a straggletag and tells me she's sorry for me for being so plain, but I know I am pretty because my hair is the colour the lake goes when the sun leans on it. Pa Mountberry says it's my mane and calls me Lottie Lion. He has fair hair like shouting straw. When I asked Ma Mountberry if he was a lion too, she lifted her hand to me.

"Don't fret, Emmie," I say, though I frown inside. A scarlet cloak lady is singing with a drummer, but her voice is a limping thing that scratches me. "Listen to that row that lady is making, yet plenty are giving her coins. Let's sing the primrose song – we're bound to get a ha'penny." I lead Emmie away from the booth. We hold hands tight as we can. I start because I find the songs. When we're at the willow brook and we sit so still the kingfisher comes or when I breath the bluebell wood in as deep as my toes, the songs drop on me like feathers, so many I can't keep them all in my head. Pa Mountberry is teaching me to write them down. He calls me a marvel, but only when Ma Mountberry can't hear him. We sing the primrose song and folk go quiet and listening and ladies dab at their eyes and toss coins at our feet.

Come dance with me, come dance, Joseph Jones did say,
But the maidens laughed at him, and he did turn away.
He walked a wood and a valley and a dell and found a primrose silver
He plucked it, put it in his pocket, and found he could dance a river.
The maidens ceased their sneers and held out their hands to him
And they danced through the winds and the night till the stars were dim.

Come dance with us, Joseph Jones, the maidens did call.
For he danced a wish and a spell, and they were in his thrall.
Strange music came that night, it bloomed from a far-off land,
A fairy maid with silver eyes came and took his hand.
'Come live with me, Joseph Jones, in the forever halls,
You shall be my love and the finest dancer at my balls.'

Three nights, they met, three nights when the moon did sing,
And in the marble forest Joseph Jones gave her a wedding ring.
Her slippers were jewels, her dress was spun from a comet's tail,
Her hair was summer and wind, her eyes were stars beneath her veil.
They danced under cloud-bloom trees and in the sunset tower,
Faster and finer than all the fairy court cos of his silver flower.

They danced till the stars sighed and the moon did yawn,
They slept on a bed of stardust guarded by a silver fawn.
'Come dance with me, my love' she said when morning came,
But his feet were clumsy and slow, and he hung his head in shame.
He reached into his pocket, but the silver primrose had wilted
His fairy bride cried pearls from her eyes, fled and he was jilted.

Cast out was he from the sunset tower and the forever halls,
Never again would he dance with his bride at the fairy balls.
And though he looked for a silver primrose until his twilight years
In wood, valley, hill, and dell he found only a handful of pearl tears
And now he sits in his cold dark room, and he hears the fairy music soar,
But poor Joseph Jones, he can dance no more. He can dance no more.

"Where did you learn that song?" a tall lady asks. The wind is in her bonnet.

"Lottie made it – it's her own," Emmie says. And the lady looks at me half doubting while Emmie scoops and counts the coins. "Gingerbread." And we push and elbow our way back to the booth. My belly grumbles. I link arms with Emmie. The queue is longer now, long as a taunt or a tickle. My feet are sore in my shoes and I long to kick them off and go barefoot. Suddenly, there's a slurred shout followed by a lot of murmur about the wrestling. The folk in front scurry off and there's nothing between us and the gingerbread. Emmie holds out a ha'penny to the lady with hair the colour of wren wings. We buy two pieces each.

"Let's sit by the White Horse," I say. A tiredness has grown wide and long in me almost filling me up. We slow weave through the crowds, past the donkeys stirring for their race with their eyes so big and sad and their ears so soft and flopping it makes my heart sore. Someone is playing a sorrowful fiddle and it wafts over to us like supper smells. Then the edge of the hill is under our feet, and down there shines the White Horse of Uffington. Only from here it's not a horse at all, but curve and stretch and white, white, white. Pa Mountberry said folk made it new again yesterday. We slow step down the slope, past the canoodlers who murmur, past the boys play fighting, and we sit close to the head. Chalk pieces are all under us. A black beetle crawls over my shoe. I eat my gingerbread swiftly because sleepiness is starting in me. Emmie gobbles hers and lays back in the grass. Her face is all drift and dream.

"Don't forget to wake me," she says, but I don't want her to sleep.

"I'm going to stand on the White Horse's eye."

"You can't," she startles. But I'm up and quick and looking back at her. Then I step onto the eye. I'm dropped into silence. Silence goes through me and out the other side of me and coldness comes up the hill and I see no one and I hear no one. Clouds fast and twist and thick and fall. Winds taste of hurt and I try to spit them out of me.

Sunset crawling and crawling and crawling in the wrong place, on the wrong side. Sunset comes up the hill, fast and changing into dark and stars. Stars in wrong shapes. Shapes I don't know. A beating in the ground.

"Emmie! Emmie!" I shout. A hand on mine. Pulling me. I fall. And then I'm clutching her and the sun is hot on my wet face and the canoodlers are staring and day is holding us. "Where did you go?"

"I never went anywhere."

Chapter Two

Six years later.

My heart is quavers. Semi quavers. Demi semi quavers. For I have seen that gentleman before – he has come for my fortepiano, come to take it away. My fortepiano with its notes as soft as a cloud's dream. My fortepiano where I took the songs I found in the bluebell gloaming and the willow way. Pa Mountberry's gift, for all lions need a kingdom, he told me, and this was mine. And so I named it Oricala. All musical instruments are kingdoms with their rivers carrying into seas and creatures in their deeps. I am still Lottie Lion when I play, my golden mane loose down my back. Though no one calls me that now. Not since Pa Mountberry died under the wings of winter. Not even my Emmie on our night walks when the moon is remembering and the darkness smells of our childhood wishes.

The gentleman nods at me as his coach passes. His eyes flash, and I run. I run the oak shadows, the green winds, the winding drive, through the great doors, into the echoing hall, and up stairs and stairs and stairs. Oricala, my fortepiano, shines back the noon sun. I sit, close my eyes, rest my hands on the keyboard, and play a frozen stream thawing into spring. My heart steadies into crochets. Emmie forced Lady Mountberry to let Oricala stay by threatening to marry a pig farmer with ruddy cheeks, a smock down to his knees, and a Berkshire burr as broad and warm as a steaming cowpat. And so Lady Mountberry relented, though her face was sour enough to curdle clouds when the other ladies asked to hear me play. How she furied when they clutched my hands, their faces wet with tears, and they murmured about their souls taking flight. And when one of her favoured ladies told her I'd grown into a beauty, it took all her willpower to keep her head from swivelling. But that was before Emmie's debut. Before Emmie met Lord Edward Finch. A man with a laugh that feels like drowsing. I would not go so far as to call him dull, but if he were running away from a bear, he would flee in 4/4 time. He is decidedly moderato. Whereas my Emmie is a crescendo climbing into octaves that Lord Edward Finch cannot hear.

There are light footsteps, then a pause, and then that prickle in me, that prickle from Lady Mountberry's stare. But I don't turn to meet her nettle gaze. I play faster, fast enough to outrun her if the keyboard was a path chasing into pine woods dark with ravens and hiding places. But the prickle is still there, so I slow into Pa Mountberry's song. The song I found when he showed me stars through his telescope: Ursa Major, the she-bear who holds the heavens on her back, and Orion who shakes his club at the gods. The golden smudge was a comet, he said. And so I ran to Oricala and I played the comet's path past Jupiter and Saturn and out to the stars no one had named. I told Pa Mountberry he was riding the comet's tail.

The last note softens into silence. I turn. Nettles. How little she looks like her portraits now.

"I saw him, Lady Mountberry. The gentleman from Luperes. He passed me in his coach."

"I make no concealment of it. He was here to conduct an evaluation." She moves into the room, sunlight picking out the grey in her chestnut ringlets, and she rests her hand on Oricala.

"You promised."

"Yes, I gave in to Emmeline's childish threats. But tell me, do you really think she'll pass over Lord Edward Finch? You must see how besotted she is – she runs to him as she used to run to you." She moves to the window, faces the green and the sun. "I can see the two of you now, tumbling and grass-stained, fists of buttercups, and Emmeline's hair falling loose. 'See the difference in our girl', Robert said. And I did. She even sounded like you. Robert spoke of that day, the day he brought you here, as a beginning, but it wasn't a beginning for me, Lottie Lion. He ought never to have asked me to be a mother to you."

"I had a mother."

"Tell me, what was she? A hop picker? A lavender girl?" The sun is burrowing in her features.

"Pa Mountberry…"

"Lord Mountberry, to you."

"He wasn't Lord Mountberry to me."

"Would you believe me if I told you, before you came, I never had the slightest suspicion? Certain behaviours are to be expected from men, but not my Robert. So, I lived in a happiness that wasn't mine, for you took those days away from me. Those days were never as I lived them. And then you took Robert away from me, too. He thought poorly of me because I could not love you, because I could not take pleasure in your gift, in your music. 'Have you ever heard anything like her,' he would say, but the fortepiano pained me. I would that I could have taken an axe to it." She presses her hands together.

"I tried to please you. When I was a child. I used to brush my hair until my arms hurt to make it gleam like Emmeline's, though it never had the shine of hers. And when the sun was dazzling and the oaks cast black shapes on the lawn, I used to make myself sit in the shade to pale my skin, but no shadows were ever thick enough to make me as fair as Emmie. And I used to stand at the looking glass, searching for what it was that made you hate me. But all I saw was myself. So, I stopped trying for a kind word or glance."

"Tell me, what do you see now when you stand at the looking glass?" She turns, and her eyes are like a chord of wrong notes jarring me.

"I do not understand."

"You must see that you are a lady now. Though you adorn yourself with frippery, it becomes you. And though you have not Emmeline's delicacy of feature or figure, you are handsome. No one who looks upon you would ever see the child that you once were. But I do. A straggletag clinging to Robert's sleeve. Dried mud on your hem. I could see your hair was flaxen under the dirt, but I thought it could never wash clean. And there was Robert pushing you towards me with a gentle hand, stroking your head and not shuddering at the grime. You held a buttercup, but you did not give it to me."

"I'd never seen a girl like Emmie before. I wanted to give her sunshine."

"She was content with me before you came."

"I didn't take her from you." Though, perhaps I did. For it was always us, out in the green, in the willow winds and the butterflies, and Lady Mountberry a pale face at a window, watching and watching. "Is that why you wish to get rid of Oricala? To punish me?" And I feel the old days brimming in me like unspent songs, Pa Mountberry next to me on the stool, his smell of brass and saddles, and him picking out a merry tune on the keyboard and me playing it back at a gallop, fast as Chesterton his mare. There is a tugging at my heart. If only days could repeat like verses and come to us again.

"You never knew how I wished I could send you back where you came from. What it took for me to tolerate you – even after Robert died, I kept you here. You have received the same education as Emmeline, though you have no appreciation of it. But you will appreciate it now."

"Mama?" Emmie's voice carries over me, lifts me. I turn.

"She intends to sell Oricala," I say, and then Emmie is beside me, her arm around me, her hair cool on my cheek. I feel tears coming but I hold them inside.

"Is that true, Mama?" A pause stretches thin while Lady Mountberry, her face all banners and bile, looks long at Emmie. The outside beats through the windows and our shadows go stale. It feels she will never speak. "Well?" Emmie says.

"The men from Luperes will be here a week Friday."

"Ten days! Not so soon, please." But I say nothing more because Emmie is standing, is facing Lady Mountberry, her eyes all shine and fury. There is a tide in her silence, and it pulls the room towards her. When I was named Lottie Lion, I tried to find an animal fitting for Emmie, for the winter of her colouring and the gentleness of her heart. But there was none, even when I imagined the creatures that dwelled on distant stars.

"Do not look at me so, Emmeline."

"I will look at you as I see you, Mama."

"If you believe that your disappointment in me can influence me, you are mistaken. Your father's disappointment was my constant companion." But she turns from Emmie and her hand flutters.

"It is cruel, Mama. And you know that Lottie needs Oricala to compose. She has her commissions."

"Five Easter hymns," Lady Mountberry laughs, and it stings me. I wrote the dawn and the blackbird and the bud into those hymns.

"I will have others. I am earning a little. Would you allow me to purchase Oricala from you?"

"At a ha'penny a month?" She raises her eyebrows at me.

"I cannot be here without Oricala. Pa Mountberry's gift to me. To me. You cannot take it." My voice is funnelling out of me and I am up, and I am striding to her. I want to seize her, her soft arms, and I want to dig my fingernails in. Then Emmie has me by my shoulders, her cool hands.

"Tell me, Lottie, you refuse to stay here without Oricala?" Lady Mountberry is pushing her face close to mine. I smell marchpane on her breath.

"Yes," I say. My face is wet. I am begging her with my eyes. She looks long at me as if she is accessing, and a hope begins to grow in me, like the change from the starless night of D Minor into D Major: she will let me keep Oricala, and I will become a great composer, and Pa Mountberry, though he is in heaven now, he will be proud of me. And Lady Mountberry and I? Perhaps we will find a peace between us. She takes steps backwards. A slow smile.

"Then you will not be here without Oricala."

"Thank you, Lady Mountberry." I lean against Emmie.

"You misunderstand. You will not be here." Her words hang. "I have found a position for you. A governess position."

"A governess position?" I'm gasping.

"I have found two. You may choose between them."

"What do you mean by this, Mama?" Emmie is holding me up.

"Truro or Uffington?" she asks. There is a spinning in me and a wrench. To leave? To leave? Even when I dreamt of being a great composer, I was always here, in Elderford, in Pa Mountberry's home, where his memory is so living, it is as if he is just behind another door. "Truro or Uffington?" she repeats. But one is not so far, not so far from Emmie, from our willow brook and primrose songs.

"Uffington," I say.

Chapter Three

Do houses have natural habitats? Like brown bears favour the Russian forests and azure-winged magpies the Spanish skies? Moorvale House's natural habitat is night – and not just any night, but one when the moon has whittled to nothing and the stars sting. How fortunate that I am arriving in the gilded September sun under the last swallows of summer. If there were a shadow large enough, Moorvale would scurry away and hide, but there is no shadow and we have to face each other instead. But, of course, it doesn't see me, it looks only at the White Horse on the hills. The windows are battlements between turrets and, though the house is symmetrical and vast, it has a crouching feeling as if it's half folded up. A white face at a window watches me. Or does she watch the White Horse? There is something in her countenance that creeps up my spine. Then she's gone, and the glass only blinks back the sunlight. The wind is in my bonnet: it smells of chalk and lavender. I can't help but turn to look at the White Horse, all startle white and stretched strange. And while I'm gawping and remembering, though trying not to remember, I hear the door open.

"Miss Chant?" the housekeeper says. I nod, though it is a strange name for me to wear and feels as full of pins as an unfinished frock. "I'm Miss Drellop. The master wasn't expecting you until this evening." Under her grey hair, her face is pickled joylessness. She is a woman who has spent her life in the key of C Minor. I beam my biggest G Major smile at her until she blanches. I will not begin by apologising. "Follow me. Leave your bags. They'll bring them." She turns. I step through the doorway into a gloom that feels like listening. Great blocks of sunlight stretch from the windows, and between them is a darkness that could stick to you. There is grandeur here in velvet and archway, but it all smells of mourning, and it catches me, and I fix my gaze on the housekeeper's narrow back, to stop my eyes from pricking, to stop from remembering tugging at my Ma's cold hand.

We pause at a door. Miss Drellop knocks but doesn't wait for an answer. And then we are inside, facing a girl dressed in black. No, not dressed in black, being gobbled up by black. As if black is a monster that has her in its jaws, and I want to pull her free, but she is not Emmie and I am not Lottie Lion now. Her hair is the colour of a weasel that has gorged on berries and slept too long in the sun. There is weasel in her eyes, too, though they are swollen. I know there will be tears in her voice when she speaks.

"Well, Prudence, stand and introduce yourself. You have French lessons to commence with, you can't continue this idling," Miss Drellop says. If ever there was a housekeeper in need of a bath consisting of stag beetles, it is she.

"Let the child be. There is nothing to be gained by French or by sums at this stage of the afternoon." I don't look at Miss Drellop. Instead, I beckon the girl to the window. "There is a glorious day out there, Prudence. The wind is chasing the starlings round that single cloud. The sunshine is thicker than honey. You could collect it in a jar and spread it on your toast. Take your book…"

"My book?" Her voice is sore from crying.

"I knew you were a reader the moment I glimpsed you. I am your governess now, and your task for today is to take your book and go and read under that oak — the one large enough to hold a warship in its branches. Though I fear you will camouflage into the shadows and we will lose you."

"May I?" She wavers. I nod. She scoops up a book and flees. Her footsteps are quavers through the corridors. I turn back to the window, to the green and gold.

"The child needs discipline, not pandering." Miss Drellop moves to my side. I do not turn my head to look at her, but her disapproval wafts over me like a stench I cannot help but breathe. I see Prudence run, dark and fast, to the oak. She sits in a cradle of roots. Her book is open. I cannot see her features, so I remember the peace on Emmie's face when she was tucked in her beloved books. For my Emmie read like the moon sails the sky. There is a pinch at my heart. And suddenly, a melody begins in me, a whisper in E Minor. I look over the grounds, the oak tops and starling flocks, up the hill to the White Horse, and the tune alters — strange notes fall and rise. There is a chill in me. And the beginning of a remembering. I push it away.

"A child of twelve needs to be outside in the sun," I say.

"You have only met Miss Prudence this very moment. How can you speak of her with any authority?"

"That may be so, but I have known bereaved children." I will not tell her of my ma.

"I have known Miss Prudence since her infancy."

"Then perhaps you could show a little softness towards her."

"And what will tomorrow's lessons be, Miss Chant? Will you send her to read under a beech tree or a willow?" She turns and I follow her again. Her footsteps sound disgruntled. I match them with my own.

I am surprised the sun even shines on Moorvale. It is a sanctuary for shadows as if they had been herded inside by a shaggy dog or summoned by a piper's tune. I never knew a house could contain so much darkness. Perhaps this family has been collecting it for generations. Perhaps this gloom that slides over me is from the age of heroes, of Arthur and his round table. And as if she can hear my thoughts, Miss Drellop starts with the history.

"You will not find another family so old. There have been Selwyns in the Vale of Uffington since long before the Normans," she says. And I believe her, for we walk in the gloom of antiquity. "Though I expect you have not heard of them, not being from these parts." But I am from these parts. At least, my ma was. I was taught to squeeze the Berkshire burr from my voice, to wring it out. But Ma's was so warm there was a summer in her words. She had a dancing way in her walk, so that folk would watch her though she was not a beauty. She smelled of strawberries steaming to jam. 'Take care not to fall asleep in the fields, for the fairies who paint the flowers will mistake you for a poppy and paint you,' she would laugh, and I would run, daisy deep, until I ran out of meadow.

"Were you listening to me, Miss Chant?" Drellop says. We have stopped at a closed door. She knocks. A low voice tells us to enter. And so, we do. The master is a dark figure at a window, turned away from us. Perhaps he watches Prudence reading under the oak? There are papers on a desk, and instruments for studying the stars, and for a moment I forget where I am or what I have become, and I expect Pa Mountberry to beckon me to a telescope and the sky to show me Jupiter.

"Miss Chant, the governess," she introduces me with so much meaning in her voice. But before I can glare at her, he turns. He turns, and it feels as if the room turns around him. He is a type of handsomeness that could only dwell in a kingdom of shadows. Perhaps they have gathered here as his worshipful subjects? Perhaps they bow and curtsy to him as he strides the corridors? His hair is dark as his shadow that stretches towards us. I shiver when it touches me. Such a man would never attend the balls to which I dragged Emmie: the two of us a whirl of candlelight and ribbons, me hurrying her into a Scotch reel, she the lightest step in the dance. You don't put a raven in an aviary. It would devour the hummingbirds. His eyes are the colour of the lowest note sustained by a bass. And when they meet mine, music crashes through me. Notes turns to chords turn to waves. I ache from my feet to my fingertips to press the music out of me, press it into a keyboard. But Oricala is gone. And so the music furies inside me.

"Miss Chant," he says. "You are pale. Do you need to sit?" I try to shake my head. There is too much music in me for me to speak. My thoughts are minims flustering into arpeggios. He has taken my arm and steered me into a chair. He has let go but his handprint leaves a warmth in my arm. He steps back. Looks down at me. There is concern in his gaze. And something of the raven in the aviary. "The journey has tired you, Miss Chant. We are a long way from Chesterfield. And after hours of road, being greeted by Drellop's unique warmth has rendered you insensible. I take it she's informed you of the family's illustrious history. She would maintain my forefathers were here before the hills."

"Yours must be the oldest family in England, if not the world," I say. There is amusement in his eyes, and it emboldens me. "And was Miss Drellop with your family from its beginnings?" I ask. He laughs. I can't help but smile.

"Have you noticed Prudence?" she starts. I want to tread on her toes.

"I did not mistake my daughter for a peculiar and enormous toadstool."

"It seems lessons in Derbyshire must be of a different order." If she pinches her lips together any tighter, they'll spring right off her face.

"Ignore her, Miss Chant. It was a great disappointment to her that Prudence's first words weren't ancient Greek. Not that she would have recognised them."

"Someone has to take your daughter's education seriously."

"Have no fear. It will take more than an afternoon below an oak to transform her into a yokel. And as for the book? Blame her love of reading on her mother. You could remove her from the library, but never the library from her. How she remembered every word she read." He turns from us then. But I can see grief outlined in his shoulders. I sit in his silence. I breathe it in. And I wonder about the raven's bride, the queen of this realm of shadows. There is a feeling in me close to jealousy. I realise I am waiting for him to turn to look at me to talk to me. But he doesn't. Drellop nudges me. We are dismissed. We are to leave. I ease myself from the chair slowly so that the leather doesn't creak. Then we are through the doorway. We are walking again, and when we turn the corner and are out of earshot, she speaks.

"The master rarely leaves his study. Though he does visit the library, her library. He can be close to her among her books. Take care he does not find you there for he will not be pleased. He keeps everything as she left it: the opened books, the piled books." I want her to lead me there. I want to trespass. I want to read Lady Selwyn's books and find her within their pages. "It is to be expected, of course. She has not been gone four months. And he worshipped her, had done since he was a boy. He took to the stars for her. He found stars with blazing tails and named them after her." She walks faster. I hurry to keep up. She pauses at a door and turns the handle. It stays shut. She nods in approval. "The west wing was hers. It is locked to all now. Even Prudence." There is a warning in her voice as if she knows I would sneak inside. We walk on. Shadows and shadows and shadows. Until finally, we stop opposite a portrait of a grand lady. I startle. I am certain she is the white face that watched me from the window. Who is she? "Did you ever see anyone more beautiful?" Drellop says.

"No," I answer truthfully. Her hair cascades. Her eyes dazzle. Her figure is a statue. Her expression is triumph. Her dress with its rich tones and embellishments would overwhelm a plainer woman. And we are all plainer women. She has winter colouring like Emmie, but while Emmie is the winter of frost-jewelled fields and robin prints in snow, this lady is the always winter of mountains arching into the heavens. How dull I feel by comparison. If she is midnight with its moonlight and mystery, I am the middle of the afternoon. I read the name 'Faith.' "Who is she?" I ask.

"The master's wife," Drellop says.

Chapter Four

Night is a different species here. At Elderford, night was clawless. It walked on padded paws through my bedroom, past my compositions with their drying ink, past Emmie's books lent to me in vain, past my dresses hanging waiting for balls, and further out. Out past the stables where the horses snored in gentle sleep, out past the willow brook silver in the woods. But at Moorvale, stick your foot out of your bed and the night will scratch your toes. It prowls by my small desk, my cold fireplace, my window that lets in gusts, my narrow bed. It does not keep me company as I lay sleepless. And a loneliness grows in me. Does Emmie miss me as I miss her? Our last morning together was just as our first, all those years ago. We didn't talk, we let the willow brook speak for us with its babble and the trees with their rustlings and the deer with its quiet step. And we took off our shoes and walked in the cool water. But then there was the coach and Emmie holding me tight and tight, and Lady Mountberry watching, a celebration in her eyes. Is she content now she has got rid of me? She has poached in bitterness all these years - she must be done by now.

Morning has come to my curtains. I inch out of bed. My feet chill on the thin rug. In the gruel light, I see my governess dress hanging. It looks as if it was stitched together with grammar, not thread. Perhaps it can teach without me? It must enjoy Latin more than I do. I favoured kitchen learning to books. Though Lady Mountberry called it my low nature showing when I sneaked away to roll pastry or knead bread. A puff of flour or powdered sugar tickling your nose is worth far more than Latin. Latin names for flowers sound like ailments that would puzzle a courtyard of doctors. Perhaps I would have been better as a cook than as a governess?

There I am in the grey mirror - how this dress makes a drab of me! If only I had a scarlet ribbon for my hair. I can't help but wonder how the master sees me. Does he see me? There is a shiver in me when I remember meeting his eyes. And then the music begins again in waves and whirls, filling me from my toes to my brow until it hurts that I cannot play it out. And I am up and into the corridor and looking and looking until I am in a music room and a fortepiano is waiting in the gloam.

I only mean to sit. I only mean to rest my fingers on the keys. I only mean to press the keys so softly no sound comes. But then the music is fast in my hands, flowing out of them and I cannot stop it. Quavers swarm. Chords stampede. G Minor sorrows. G Major comforts. The melody is in the walls. Too loud. Too loud. And yet I don't stop. There is more and more and more. I don't know if I'm breathing. I don't know if I'm listening. I don't know if I'm feeling my hands. The music hurtles and takes me with it: tumbling and tumbling and tumbling. Then a sound in the doorway. I drop my hands. I stumble to my feet. The master. The raven in the aviary.

"I'm sorry. I only intended to prepare Miss Selwyn's music lesson," I say. He stays in the doorway. I try to read his expression. Is he angry? Will I be dismissed from Moorvale? And where will I go? There is a sinking in me. But I hold my head up. And when my gaze meets his, there is music in me.

"Keep playing," he says. So, I do. And he watches me. He watches me through the proud crotchets, the swooning arpeggios, the solemn semibreves. And I wonder if I will ever find these melodies again. They rush from me and then they are gone. Silence rings out.

"I've never heard anything like it," he says. And then he is beside the fortepiano. I look up at him. "Who wrote that music?"

"I did," I say. "Though I haven't written it down, yet. And I fear I won't remember all the notes, and it'll end up patchworks and missing pieces." And I remember Pa Mountberry scribbling on sheet music, fast as he could, the stave splodged with ink, the triplets a scrawl, while I played a riot in E Major. I named the piece "Sonata in the Lion's Den."

"How terrible to think I will never hear it again," he says. But there is no amusement in his eyes.

"I do lose music. When I don't write it down swiftly enough, though I prefer to think of it as mislaid, as if it I might discover it in the bottom of a wardrobe."

"And have you ever found music in your wardrobe?"

"Not yet. But perhaps I never looked diligently enough. I was too busy gathering it from the woods."

"How I have missed out all these years. I've never found so much as a jig in the woods. Unless thunder counts as music."

"I'm sorry to tell you it doesn't. But there is music everywhere. I'll show you." I rise, move to the window, and open the curtains. Morning washes me. I blink at the sunlight. There is no White Horse - we are on the other side of the house. I find I am relieved. And then he is by my side. His arm almost touching mine. We share a silence. A silence I could languish within. We look at the long shadows of the yew trees, and the fields beyond sprinkled with chalk. The bustard birds are dancing.

"I hear nothing," he says.

"See those fat clouds, not the wispy ones, but the ones that look like they've over indulged at a summer fair and are too inebriated to find their way home. Look at them bumbling along. The wind isn't strong enough to hurry them." I let the music come to me. "F Major. Largo. It begins in a high octave."

"If only I had kept to my music studies, then I might understand you." He smiles. His arm is pressed against mine. I feel it all through me.

"I'll play it for you." I rush to the fortepiano. And I play the clouds, their weighty bellies, their sleepy path. And he is near me.

Watching me, whenever I raise my head. He is more handsome than I realised, and he was already too handsome. I struggle to keep to the clouds. Other music is stirring in me. I should stop, but I don't. I hold his gaze, and I let the darker music come. And when it is done, and my hands are silent and aching, he looks long at me.

"I believe, one day, I shall boast that I knew you, Miss Chant." There is something in his eyes close to tenderness.

"Call me Charlotte," I say. I am not Miss Chant, the governess, when I am at the fortepiano, even when it is not Oricala.

"Charlotte." How my name sounds in his voice. I never wanted to be anyone other than Lottie Lion before, but now? I want him to say it again. "One day, many years from now, you will be a great composer celebrated in the royal houses of Europe. Even in Germany, and we know how they regard our music. And I? I will be an elderly man with grey hair and a stooping back in the audience telling the poor fellows next to me that I once knew you. And they will think it a great misfortune to be seated near a bore. And they won't believe me."

Suddenly, he looks past me to the doorway. I turn, and there is Prudence. She looks at me with fury. Her pointy chin wibbles. Her thin fingers flex. Her amber eyes snap. How long has she been watching us? Her step is quiet; and my playing is loud. There is so much more weasel in her now she is angry. I almost fear being bitten. I brace. There is a silence that feels like pinching. Then, she turns and runs.

"That will be all, Miss Chant," the master says.

So, I'm Miss Chant again. Governess. But a governess without a student. For Prudence will not come out of her room, will not open her door to me.

"No lessons beneath the oak today," Drellop says. Her smirk stings me. There is mockery in her stride. What am I to do now? The shadows stifle me. I'm wading through them, tasting them, breathing them. And then I'm through the final door and outside and blinking. I want to cut the sunshine into great sheets and sew it into a frock and stride Moorvale's corridors until the shadows wither.

I walk. Summer is taking its last breath. There is sorrow in the waning gold, in the slowing bees, in the cooling winds. When I was a girl with dandelion wishes in my hair, I used to fear summer would never return. That the swallows would carry its soul to Egypt, to rest with pharaohs and cats. There are starling flocks moving over me in the shapes of galaxies. Galaxies Pa Mountberry showed me. My heart pangs. My vision blurs.

"Mind where you go, Miss," a man says. I rub my eyes. He has whiskers going grey, skin so ruddy it looks uncooked, and a Berkshire burr that could turn skimmed milk to cheddar. "Heard Selwyn was getting a new governess." He looks at me as if evaluating the price I would fetch at market. I wonder if he's comparing me to the master's wife, and as if he can read my thoughts, he says, "terrible, terrible. There won't be another like her."

"What happened to her?" The words are out of me before I can stop them.

"Same as what happened to the rest of the Lady Selwyns. The Lord's wife, his mother, his grandmother, and all those before them. All going back to I don't know how long ago. I can still see his mother, that Lady Selwyn, out on the hills in her nightgown, her face terrible wild. The wind was tangling her hair, and her feet were bare. She clutched at me. She called me names that weren't mine. She told me the White Lady was coming for her."

"White Lady?"

"Not from these parts, are you?" He pauses as if expecting an apology. When none comes, he continues. "That White Horse on the hill – terrible old it is. Goes back to the time before there were men here, before there were men at all."

"Then who could have made it?"

"The White Horse wasn't made, it was ridden. In the old times, before men, the other folk rode across this land on their white horses. Big as that one there." He points to the hill as if I need reminding. I find myself looking at it, anyway. He moves closer. He smells of polished wood and spaniels sleeping by the fire. "The other folk didn't live here. They lived in an elsewhere. A place where the sun didn't rise and set like ours but waxed and waned like the moon. Strange things grew under that sickle sun – all ice." He pauses to rub his eyes. And I picture another sky, paler than ours, with a thin sliver of sun. A chill begins in me. I wish I had a cloak. "The other folk could only travel from there to here on their horses. Well, the White Lady's horse lamed itself on that hill and died, and she could never get back home again. She sat and waited. And in the end, men came, and she married one, and bore him daughters. But she couldn't settle, and she couldn't get old, and she couldn't die. The only thing she could do was mourn." He pauses to scratch his whiskers. The wind is beside us. "The White Lady mourned until she was a wraith. But she still couldn't get home. She's still out there. If the fog comes, so will she. And mind she doesn't mistake you for one of her daughters, or her daughters' daughters. Cos if she does, she'll take you and she won't let go. And she'll claw at you and wail and pull at your hair and fill you with her grief. And you'll pine for a home that wasn't yours. Until you become a wraith." I shiver all through me. The wind is in my hair. He steps back. Then he laughs from his belly. "The face on you. You don't have anything to fear. Not unless you've seen the sun setting in the north."

"The sun setting in the north?"

"Don't go working yourself into a fret. It's not possible. That's how you know you'll be safe." But there's a spinning in me and a remembering. I was small and I stood on the horse's eye and I saw. I saw. "She comes to those who see the sun set in the north."

Chapter Five

I have become a cartographer of silence. My days are maps of its terrains. And there are so many terrains of silence. Prudence ignoring me, my instructions, my questions. Her hands in her lap. Her eyes lowered. Her brow smooth insolence. This is a punishing silence. Then there's the silence when she lifts her pen, dips it in the ink well, and slowly puts nib to paper. She looks up at me. I wait. Then, she puts her pen down. This is a taunting silence. There's the silence of Drellop lurking in the corridor outside our lessons, her narrow back turned to me, but with listening in her shoulders. This is a triumphant silence. And all these terrains are hostile. But there's another – when the master passes me in the hallway, and he doesn't speak or nod, but he looks at me, he looks at me. Or when I'm walking and I take off my bonnet to let the wind in my hair, and I feel a shiver and turn and there he is at a window. Our eyes meet and I feel it all through me. What kind of silence is this? What kind of terrain is this? I do not know. But it is dark, is tangled, is pathless. There's a beckoning in it and a warning. And it brings me melodies that I write out late at night into the wolf hours.

And there's another silence that pains me. Emmie's. Still no letter, though I've been at Moorvale three weeks. This terrain is loneliness. And though I first travelled here as a child when I lost my ma, now the moors are vaster and stretch out and out with no valley or river or violet wood. I was once a girl with daisies in my pockets, with a sister who wrote stories for me when I was sad. I read them now. I see the smudges my long-ago tears made on the pages. Lady Mountberry thought my sorrow a catching thing, but Emmie wanted to give me smiles. And so she did with a lion who turned into a fortepiano and chased an orchestra. And with a princess doomed to wed a wicked king who escaped in a pair of slippers made from smoke. Best of all was the peasant boy who found a golden acorn – he planted it and it grew into a castle and in each room was a cloud that rained sweetmeats and flowers. This story became a game, became a hope. For we had whole days in acorn drifts. Whole nights in buttercup dreams. We stole sugared almonds and pretended they dropped from clouds.

But there's another silence. And it comes with a coldness. Coldness that stings. Stings me awake. For this is a silence I dream. I dream I'm a girl again and all is high up and whipping winds and kestrels diving and laughter soaring, and I feel sun hot on my face and I smell ale spilled on grass and I taste gingerbread. And there's Emmie laying down in cowslips and blue butterflies. She closes her eyes. A black beetle crawls. There's chalk white and white and white. I step on it. The silence comes. It roots me, coils into me. I cannot move. I cannot cry out. And there is a sunset wrong and a darkness behind it and I must wake before it touches me. I fight and fight. I wake a shivering thing. This terrain is terror. And as I walk the corridors of Moorvale I try not to think of the story of the White Lady. I try not to remember the sun setting in the north.

"Miss Chant, did you hear me?" I startle. "No doubt the music that fills your existence drowned me out." The raven. The master. Why is he always more handsome than I remember? I catch sight of my reflection in the looking glass behind him – meek and grey – a collared dove of a woman. "Well, am I to employ a trumpeter to announce me? Just so that I may have your attention?" He smiles. If I forget my appearance, I might be able to answer him.

"I was simply preoccupied with my plans for Prudence's lessons." My heartbeat is all through me. I don't know what to do with my hands.

"I believe I was better off before I met you. Before I knew the world was filled with music I cannot hear. Now, when I ride out past the fields and I see how autumn is starting on the woods, I think of you and how you would hear them. What is the music of the oaks as they turn golden? Will you play it for me?"

"I have not met your oaks, so I do not even know if their music is in a minor key or a major key or moderato or appassionato."

"Come with me. There are so many places I wish to show you. We're not just those hills and that horse. Though they are all anyone knows of us. Come with me, Charlotte, and afterwards, play to me." He holds out a hand. I want him to take mine. I want him to take me to the golden woods. Music thrums through me. There's a warning in it.

"I cannot." I step past him and down the corridor.

Prudence. How curious it is to recall I wished to help her, now we battle, now I want to conquer, now I worry she will vanquish me. Through the doorway, I see her sitting at the table. Her hands are folded in her lap. Her countenance is benign. I enter.

I stumble through French and, miracle of miracles, she writes. I read over her shoulder. Her handwriting is looping and confident. My lessons are too easy for her.

"My mama spoke five languages," she says as if to chide me. Of course, the raven's bride was a peerless scholar. "Her most favourite was Latin." Of course, it was. I can see Lady Selwyn at an emperor's side, the Colosseum a frame for her beauty - in the arena, gladiators battle lions and rhinoceroses and Pluto himself for a single one of her smiles. What would anyone battle for me? A fieldmouse? A dung beetle? A daddy long legs?

"From what I have observed, you have an aptitude, Prudence. I'm certain you will be able to speak five languages if you choose," I say. Her face crumples into tears.

"But my mama will never know. I could learn fifty languages, but I'll never speak with her again." And then I'm crouching, my arm around her shoulders, and she's weeping so her tears fall on her work. Great sobs shake her. Poor motherless child. She pushes me away, pushes her work on the floor.

"Would you like me to call for Miss Drellop?" I ask. She shakes her head. There's a shame in me so large I feel I cannot contain it. How could I think Prudence an enemy when she's just a girl who lost her mother? I've become what Emmie and I used to call a drackle heart.

"I want to go to the White Horse. Mama used to take me," she says. Dread pinches me. I have not been long enough from my dreams.

"I believe your father would want you to study."

"How would you know what my father wants?" Her gaze pierces me. It's a direct accusation. I turn so she cannot read what's in my face – he wants to take me to the woods. My heartbeat is in my hands. I look out of the window and rest my palms on the cold pane. Autumn breathes through the hills and fields, yet the sky is a pale rainless grey.

"Very well, Miss Selwyn."

The White Horse

We walk with the winds in our cloaks, and we don't look back. The hills. The hills. How vast they are – up and up and up. There are slow sheep, swift kestrels, tumble ways, and chalk pieces under our feet. Starling flocks swirl above us. And I remember. I remember, Emmie's hand warm in mine, the sun in Pa Mountberry's dear face, and Lady Mountberry with scorn in how she held her skirts. My heart smarts. Prudence is ahead of me.

"Not so fast, Miss Selwyn," I say. I hurry to keep up with her. My legs ache, the chalk pieces hurt through my shoes, and the wind is tugging my bonnet.

"My mama could spend whole days on the hills and never tire," she says. It is almost a challenge. Perhaps she thinks I will take the bait and wander the hills until I'm grey and rheumatic? "Her family had been here always."

"As long as Lord Selwyn's family?" I ask. She glares at me. I ought not say his name, for my voice alters.

"Longer. Her family had been here since the beginning." When was the beginning? When the Saxons buried their kings with gold, or when the other folk rode through this land? And there's something in her countenance past pride, past triumph, something that makes me shudder. There's no weasel about her now. I do not want to be here. Music whispers through me – low and haunting – making a midnight of the morning. Fear prickles me. The air churns. The sky darkens. Prudence's cloak is a black flame about her.

"The rain is coming. We must return to the house, or we'll be caught in the downpour," I say. How grateful I am to the weather. There are times when the greatest gift is an excuse.

"You promised me I could visit the White Horse." There is something of embers in her eyes. I do not like to meet her gaze. I hold my cloak in my fist and the winds wrench at it. The starlings are fast shapes far away.

"The White Horse will not rise from the hills and gallop to Timbuktu. It will be here tomorrow and all the days thereafter, and so you will be able to visit many times."

"Papa won't allow me." But she smiles.

"Why?" I ask. But she turns. "Prudence, answer me." But she walks. Her cloak is wild. Her feet are swift. The music rises and fear unfolds in me, slowing me. "Come back." Rain. I'm pelted and chilled and running after her. I slip. I steady. And I run again. I lunge, grip her arm.

"Unhand me, Miss Chant." But her voice is calm.

"Why has your father forbidden it? Tell me." I want to shake her. Rain is pouring down her face. Her cloak is wet and wilting. "Why, Prudence?" Her silence holds me, traps me, stills me. But I do not let go of her. She will run to the White Horse, and I will have to follow her, follow her to where the silence coils thick and the sun sets in the north. "Why does your father forbid it?" I ask again. But she just lifts her ember eyes and looks past me. A sly smile.

"You may ask him yourself, Miss Chant." she says. I turn. There he is striding up the hill as if there were no effort in it. His voice is in the winds, tossed about in them like a ship to its doom. Prudence is laughing. Did she have me bring her here to anger him? So that he would look at me as he does now? For there is betrayal in his glare. Gone is the way he has looked at me these past weeks, and the loss pains me. Rain soaks him, but he walks as if he doesn't feel it. And then he is near, his hand reaching for Prudence.

"Why did you bring her here? Was it your intent to torment me?" But before I can answer, he has taken her and they are off down the hill, and I am a cold and shaking thing left to walk my way back alone.

Chapter Six

Dearest Sister,

Oricala is saved! How I have longed to tell you, nay positively itched to tell you, what Edward and I were planning, but I couldn't lest Mama found out (you know she's as wily as a fox spying for the king). Edward has bought Oricala! This very afternoon, Oricala will be delivered to Arunspear. There will be no cold welcome, no strangers' fingers thudding on the keyboard. No one shall ever play Oricala but you, my darling Lottie Lion. Just as our Papa would have wished. How Mama fumes. It is a wonder she doesn't combust. She has begun to look at me as she used to look at you. I am the enemy, now. And Edward, perfect Edward. Do you understand why I love him now? He is all goodness. How you used to call him moderato! My dear sister, cease daydreaming of appassionato heroes. The novels warn against such men. If only you would read them.

How lonely Elderford is without you! And the old days are ghosts in every room. Here, in my chambers, where we whispered our secrets until the night was pushed from the sky. If only we could be girls together once more – blackberrying in the south fields or eating roasted chestnuts by the fire. Papa always burnt them. But did they not taste the better for being a little blackened?

A knock on my door. I put Emmie's letter down and wipe my eyes. I expect it is Drellop again. How she delighted in telling me Prudence would not be having lessons today. And now I have been all day in this little grey room, all day with the rain at my window, all day waiting to be dismissed from Moorvale. And now the day has dipped into evening. I open the door. It is him. I meet his eyes. I am still lion enough for that.

"Am I to leave tomorrow, Lord Selwyn?"

"Leave? No, Miss Chant. I cannot excuse my behaviour yesterday. I know you did not lead Prudence to the hill to injure me. For you could not possibly have known."

"Known what, Lord Selwyn?"

"Must you call me so?"

"How else ought I address you?"

"Caleb. Call me Caleb." There's a pause that feels like floating, then his eyes lower. "My wife was a dazzling woman. No one could equal her for wit, for understanding. But she became unwell. There were days when I had to search for her on the hills and bring her home in my arms, for she was too insensible to walk." He looks at me. I am a mingle of sympathy and jealously. There is so much hurt in his face. How I want to touch him, his cheek, his brow. I clasp my hands, so they don't betray me.

"A country gentleman I encountered when I had not been long here told me a story of a White Lady," I say. He flinches.

"Who was he?"

"He did not give me his name. He was broad and whiskered and had a merry, ruddy face. He smelt strongly of polished wood."

"That will be Wellack. Curse him. Wheel maker - but spends too many of his hours in gossip. Well, I can only wonder at the lurid tale he told you. My wife perished from brain fever. In the earlier stages, this manifested in a preoccupation with a myth about that wretched horse." He rubs his forehead. "My mother suffered also. I was no more than a boy when I lost her. She would wake me in the night, so convinced was she that the White Lady was coming, and that we had to make our escape. The last time I saw her she was leading me up the hills in a storm. In her haste, she had neglected to dress me. I was still in my night clothes. It was February. I caught a chill. For weeks, I lingered between this world and the next. By the time I'd recovered, she had gone."

"I'm so sorry, Caleb." I am touching his arm. I snatch my hand away. A melody in G Minor is winding through me, sweet and sorrowful. I ache to play it out, to play it to him.

"Why am I burdening you with my history? You came to Moorvale to teach French and sums, not to listen to a widower's lament."

"It is no burden. I lost my mother when I was a girl."

"Oh, Charlotte. I'm sorry. Did she have a genius for music?"

"She had a genius for happiness, which she shared with all who knew her." There's a soreness in my heart. And the music changes to Ma's song. The music I heard when she carried me on her hip through the poppy fields. When the world was two acres of red and green and gold. "May I play the fortepiano to you?"

He leads me by candlelight. The night divides before us as an obedient sea. Obedient to its master. And all the grandeur of Moorvale becomes gilded glimpses that, moments later, are submerged once more. I glance at him. He is even more handsome by candle glow. But candle glow can make an immortal queen of the meekest maid, so what more can it do for a raven?

"Before you play for me, there's something I wish to show you," he says, as we stop by a door. And I have a memory of Emmie, startle-eyed at a novel, gasping of horrors in closed rooms. Night is flaring up the walls and I hear it as low chords creeping louder. The candle is small. I fear it going out. "I cannot find music like you, Charlotte, but I can find stars." We enter his study. The curtains are open, and so our reflections move in the dark windows. I see myself as a wraith, while he, the raven, is crowned by stars. He gathers and piles papers on his desk. Wax falls on them. He sets the candle down. "I'm mapping the heavens," he says. "It's been a preoccupation of mine since my boyhood. I learned the constellations before I learned my letters." He smiles and I feel it all through me. "There's a comet tonight, Charlotte." He opens a window, and a breeze stirs his hair. I smell bonfires smouldering. He looks through a telescope. There's a silence that feels like a mystery and then his hand is on my arm leading me across the room, and I am at the telescope, and it is cold against my eye. I hesitate. My dreams beat through me, so I close my eyes, not wanting to look lest I see those strange stars. "Charlotte, one cannot see comets through one's eyelids." He is so close to me that I feel the warmth of him. "When I was not much more than an infant, I had a fancy that the stars were gold. I was determined that when I was grown, I would mine the very heavens." He laughs. He is even closer now. I want to lean into him. I have to open my eye to stop myself and I see through the telescope, and I see – I see the same stars Pa Mountberry showed me. Relief billows in me. What a dilly head I've become. Those other stars, the ones that don't exist – how can I be certain I ever saw them at all? I had forgotten that day for years – why ought I trust my memory now?

"And do you still intend to mine the heavens?" I ask.

"I set out for Sirius on the stroke of midnight. If my calculations are correct, it will be a six-day walk." Our eyes meet.

"My sister used to tell me a story – that the heavens were once empty. Empty but for a celestial lion who roamed until he became so old that his mane turned to dandelion wishes. He shook his mane - the wishes flew across the heavens, where they planted, and grew into stars."

"And what happened to the lion after he lost his mane?"

"My sister told me he yawned a thousand-year yawn and then went to sleep on the other side of the stars. And he slumbers there still. Be careful not to wake him on your journeys," I smile. But he doesn't smile back at me. There is appassionato in his face. I try to steady my heartbeat. How alone we are. I think he is going to touch me. He leans. He leans and takes the telescope to his eye. He is silent studying the stars, and I am all pianissimo, for it seems the heavens are waters I could disturb with my breathing and his comet could be blown afar by an uttered word.

"Charlotte," he says. And I don't answer for I want to hear him speak my name again. "Charlotte. The comet." He holds the telescope still while I lean, and I am glad, for I am all shiver. There is a golden smudge in the heavens. The night is holding its breath. All is gleam and wonder. And I hear. I hear the comet – a melody high and shining, so sweet it fills me with longing. Such music could not be played on any keyboard. Not even Oricala! It is star stuff fit only for strings spun from the comet's tail. I move back and let him take the telescope to his eye. And I don't speak for the music has filled me to my brim, so much that I find myself wiping away tears. I watch him watching the comet and there's reverence in his shoulders. He could be lighting candles on an altar. "When do you think this comet last flew over Uffington?" he says.

"I would not know if it were last Tuesday or when Jesus himself walked these lands."

"It was long, long, ago, Charlotte. Before there were men here." He does not move, though the night winds are in his hair. And I imagine this land wild and ancient. What curious beasts roamed here in the youth of the stars? "It will be millions of years before the comet passes again," he says. "Perhaps there will be no men once more and it will glide over an empty world?" A loneliness pierces me, and I close my eyes. There is just the silence of him studying the heavens. I do not stand on the edge of it – I am deeper than I could wade. Only when I hear a faint rustling, do I open my eyes. He is still at the telescope. I glance at the window, at my reflection. I gasp. Ice floods me. Fear cracks me. It is she. It is she. Behind me. The raven's bride. Her face is white, white, white. There are stars in her. Her hair is night. Her eyes are flame. Her white hand – she is raising it – she is raising it. I scream. And then he is grabbing me, his hands hurting my arms. "Charlotte. Charlotte. What's wrong?"

"It's her. It's her." I shake. His face is so close to mine. I can see the amber flecks in his brown eyes.

"Who?" His hands tighten.

"Can't you see her?" I shudder as I raise my eyes to the window, and I see, I see. Us. Only us. No white figure accusing me with her eyes, with her raised hand. I wriggle from his grip, and I face the doorway, but there is only darkness, and I rush into it, and I peer hard for a glint of dress, of hair, and I strain with listening for a step, for a rustling. But there is nothing.

Chapter Seven

My guilty conscience has a fair face and a quiet step. She follows me through the corridors, and when I stop and wait and listen, she is gone. I breathe relief. But I walk swifter to my lessons, swifter past the master's study. I do not linger for conversation when he approaches me, his eyes espressivo. I do not answer him when he calls my name, his voice dolce. For I remember her white hand raising. And fear stings me again. I am being followed now and it quickens my heart and brings sweat to my brow. I will stand firm. I will not run. A lion can better a ghost.

"Miss Chant, you scurry about the house like a squirrel." It is Drellop coming round the corner. There is something wrong with her face. I do believe she is smiling, though you would not find the contortions of her features in an encyclopaedia of smiles. Perhaps she tried smiling once or twice in her youth before deciding it was not for her? I beam a C Major grin to show her how it's done. There – she is back to her pursed lips and sour brow. "And will you be attending tonight?"

"Tonight?" I ask.

"All Hallows Eve. I trust you've been invited." But the glint in her eye betrays her: she knows full well that no one has invited me. A governess is a solitary species. But how am I to answer her without humiliation? "I am sure it is an oversight. You are more than welcome to join me. It is the custom for women to wear white dresses. I would loan you one, but none of mine would accommodate you." She pauses as if expecting an apology for my frame. I offer none. I do not lament my potato peasant figure, I only lament that I have not, this moment, returned from the fields with a bucket of potatoes to tip over her.

"Thank you, Miss Drellop. As fortune would have it, I am in possession of a white dress." I do not long to go with her, but I do not want an evening listening to the far-off sounds of merriment with a single candle for company.

"The staff are assembling in the hall at six o'clock." She nods and steps past me. There is triumph in her walk, but I do not let it smart me for I know I will look well in my white dress: my peasant dress. How Lady Mountberry smiled when Emmie and I descended the stairs. How she tied a green ribbon in my hair, put her arm around me, took me into her smell of pearls and disdain, and told me to listen, to listen – for somewhere out in the fields of Berkshire a flock of sheep was bleating and baaing and begging me to come home. How her laugh rang cruel. But then Emmie took me to the night and the coach and the ball. And we danced so swiftly the candlelight couldn't catch us.

The clock chimes six. I take a last look at the mirror. I am a governess dressed as a lady dressed as a peasant. But which am I? All three. My frock was a parting jibe from Lady Mountberry – for the fields of Berkshire. And now I will wear it in field fog and bonfire smoke, and it will lose its smell of sugar almonds and chandeliers. And what will the master see when he looks at me? The country girl I ought to have become, or the lady I once was?

I take the corridors quickly, letting my skirts fly out, and the old me runs alongside in the mirrors. I feel she will overtake and part from me. Perhaps there is a ball in the mirrorlands tonight? Perhaps she will dance until the stars sleep? Then she is gone, and I am down the stairs and Drellop is waiting, her arms folded so tightly around her cloak, I cannot spy an inch of her dress. There is shock in her face at my appearance. And displeasure. Only maids wait with her, girls my age or thereabouts. The other staff must have already departed. In the windows, night is tinted with fire. And I can smell damp and smoke and laughter. There is merriment out there and I will walk to it and be part of it. A gigue starts in me and tickles my feet.

"Doesn't Miss Chant look the lady, girls?" Drellop says.

"Princess Bo Peep," comes the snigger.

"Hush, Mary. Though perhaps there is a flock of sheep wandering about Moorvale in search of its queen." Her eyes are lit with spite.

"It is a shame I am not dressed as a shepherdess, for I should like to be in possession of a crook," I say, and I look lightning at them. The smirk falls off Mary's doughy face.

"My apologies, Miss Chant. On closer inspection, I can see you're attired as a milk maid. Would you like me to lead you to the nearest dairy?"

"I would indeed. I expect the cows would prove more amicable company."

"Wrap your cloak tightly about yourself. It is the custom to hide the white of our dresses until the allotted moment."

Then I am following Drellop and her ensemble out into the dark where there is no need for her to remind me to wrap my cloak tightly, for the wind reminds me with its black bite. And it carries laughter that makes loneliness crescendo in my chest. Why did I join them? My grey room and lone candle seem better companions, but I keep up with Drellop's swift step on the slippery path. There are stars in the puddles. There is smoke on my tongue. And I remember Ma warning me of Old Josephine who waits in water on All Hallows Eve. 'Take care you don't look into the puddles, for you shall see her – her pike teeth and her river weed hair - and in every mirror thereafter you shall see her face.' Mud splashes my hem. My dress will be stained. There are folk and folk and folk traipsing ahead of us, but I do not see the master. The hedgerows tug at my cloak. Then the path opens into a field. A great bonfire burns. The night is under embers. The villagers are fire-gilded silhouettes. I look for him in shadow figures and grinning faces.

"Mary, fetch Miss Chant some cider," Drellop says.

"Can't the lady get her own drink?" Mary says. And even I feel the weight of Drellop's glare. I watch Mary's sullen back as she disappears into the crowd. There is chatter and spice and jostle and heat. And I have a longing for blackened chestnuts. Which key is merriment? B Major? E Flat Major? Then why is a melody in C Sharp Minor rising up like a mist? And why does it make me want to turn back the way I have come?

"We are great believers in tradition here, Miss Chant," Drellop says. "And our traditions are old." She is watching the bonfire, the flames bending and crackling, the black shapes of folk. And I watch too, and the music in me shivers in high octaves, lamentoso. What is there to lament in broad farmers swilling ale, in girls giggling, in glee-faced boys darting in and out of the crowd? I clutch my cloak closer about me. And I feel the darkness outside the fire glow and the hills within it and the White Horse above, watching.

"Your cider, my lady." Mary nudges me. Still keeping my cloak tight, I take the warm cup and breathe the clove steam.

"Thank you, Mary." I take a sip. Spice on my tongue. Heat down my throat. It tastes of orchards and hearths. I drink. I lower the cup. And then I notice that Mary's cloak is open. And her dress is dark.

"Why aren't you wearing a white dress?" I ask. But she doesn't answer. Her eyes are dancing insolence. Her doughy face is struggling to contain laughter. "Weren't we all to wear white dresses?"

"Don't you have eyes, my lady?" she says. I look past her, past a group of narrow lads with grease-flattened hair furtively sharing a bottle of beer, past a shipwreck-faced man leaning on a cane and keeping ten men captive with a tale, past two little girls holding hands and trying to push closer to the fire, to three elderly ladies nattering. The bonfire glow has deepened the crags on their faces and made them older than the land itself. But they don't wear white - their dresses are black. And beside them a group of wildflower maidens jig and twirl as if a fiddler is playing. Their hair shines back the fire. And their frocks are scarlet, green, and brown.

"Miss Drellop, you told me it was the custom to wear white dresses."

"I trust you won't take offence, Miss Chant. It was only a little sport," she says. It seems I am her amusement for the evening. Mary is whispering into the ear of a lanky fellow who peers at me, his gaze brambles. I will not stay here. I will flee to my grey room, though this night will follow me and scratch me till dawn. But then I see him. The master. He is talking to a peony of a girl. She is not much older than me, and though Lady Mountberry would not regard her a beauty, I do. Is her hair chestnut or is it just the tint of the fire? Do her eyes always gleam and laugh so? Does he notice the meadow in her smile? Shadows hide his expression, yet dread pinches me as if he had taken her arm. He turns from her and moves through the crowd – slowly, for folk stop him. How they all flock to him. How unlike them he is. A raven among sparrows. Even the shadows are pulled toward him. Embers and night frame him. What is he saying to that woman who carries a wriggling toddler in her arms? She sets the boy down and he hides behind her skirts. She has something in her hands – grey lumpen fabric. She pulls it over her head. There are features marked on it in charcoal smudges. A face – eyes smearing downwards – a black hollow for a mouth. I glance at the wildflower girls – they are lifting masks, tying them in place. Long hair tangles in string. Laughter beneath cotton. Eyes blinking in holes. Sewn smiles. Those two little girls are still holding hands but now they have paper grins with too many teeth. The mother behind is stroking the smallest girl's hair – smudges for her eyes – no mouth.

"Miss Drellop, you never told me of this. Why is everyone…"

"Did I not, Miss Chant? It must have slipped my mind. How careless of me," Her voice is muffled. I turn. A wooden mask hides her face. Her eyes glint in holes. "I trust you will not be unnerved. The masks are an old tradition, but a harmless one. Even Lord Selwyn participates." But the music in me is arching is climbing is roaring. The master is lifting a wooden mask. And then he is wearing a devil face. The wood is age cracked and dark. Firelight slithers on it. He looks towards me. I take a step backwards. A hand grips my elbow. "You aren't leaving are you, Miss Chant?" Drellop says.

"Thank you for inviting me, but…" Suddenly, her hands are at my cloak, are picking at the knot. "Leave me be." I push her away. My cloak flaps open. My dress is exposed. Masked heads turn towards me. I pull my cloak about me, hide the white. The path feels far. I start.

Other hands grip my arms. A tall figure. A face of lumps. Laughter behind a black mouth. I writhe. More hands. "Let me be." My cloak is undone is torn off me is thrown. Someone has snatched it. I am let go. Drellop stands in front of me laughing behind her witch face. Wind tugs at my dress. The night is chill on my back. "Return my cloak now, Miss Drellop. You have had your game." The crowd are watching me. There is a silence that feels like talons. Then there are whispers behind the masks rising and passing and joining in one voice.

"The White Lady." A little girl points. Her smile has too many teeth.

Chapter Eight

The bonfire glow glides over Drellop's witch face – the hook nose and thrusting chin. I can see her eyes are smiling in the holes.

"How careless of you to drop your cloak," she says. "But there is a fire. You will not suffer from the cold. Not with such a crowd about you." She gestures. The night has gone still, still over the embers chasing in the winds, still over the masked faces watching me, still over the black hills and the White Horse. There are too many stars. I hug my arms. The cold is in my dress. I try not to feel it, try not to feel the fear curling in my chest. How I want to run. I see the path. She shakes her head at me. The wildflower girls are dancing again.

I inch backwards into a figure behind me. I peer up at a face of three smudges. His hands are moving up my arms. I feel the warmth of his fingers as he grips me.

"Unhand me," I say. His black smudge stare falls on me like a slithering thing. I want to shake it from me. I try to meet it with a lion glare, but I am trembling. "Unhand me, now." I try to pull free. I am iron held. Panic moves in me, opens its wings. His thick hands are bruising my arms. The masks watch me, watch him hurt me. Charcoal eyes. Sewn mouths. Too many teeth. They whisper – white lady – white lady – white lady. The fire roars.

"You want to go home?" he says. There's ale on his breath. He is bull broad. I am too small. I cannot get free.

"Yes." I will run.

"Then we shall take you home," he says. He is lifting me. The ground – I cannot feel it. My feet swing. The masks are coming to me. He is carrying me. And they are with us. The night thickens and goes cold. I cannot hear the fire. We are in the dark. Masks and masks and masks. We are moving we are climbing we are going up the hills. The stars bite. The masks whisper – white lady – white lady – white lady.

"Put me down. Put me down." Do they hear me? Am I shouting? The masks whisper. My face is wet. Eyes in holes. Looking at me. Someone carries a torch. In flickers, I see him – his devil face. Pushing through the crowd. He mustn't touch me. He calls a name. The bull man halts. They part for him. Masks turn to him. Whispers. Whispers. I push and fight, but the bull man holds me, holds me for him. The moon is on his devil face. It is in the cracks of the wood. I cannot see his eyes. He is close. He is close. He reaches for me. Someone is screaming. He has taken me. He is talking. Anger in his voice. And then he is carrying me down the hill away from the masks. Away. Away. He is talking to me, and his words are soft, but I do not know them. The stars are all over us. I think the path is beneath us. I hear his steps. I do not want him to set me down. He is listening to me, but I do not say anything. My teeth chatter, but I do not feel the cold. I lay my head against him. When did he remove his devil face? The moon silvers him. How like the raven he is. I close my eyes.

I hear a door unlocking and hinges creaking. The wind leaves us, and I smell closed curtains and portraits hanging and stairways reaching into higher darkness. He is speaking again, soft as feathers. I hear my name. A doorway. Open curtains and a silver room. I do not want to see the windows. And then I am lowered and let go and cushioned on a sofa. The moon is on him. His shadow is across the floor. He is wrapping a blanket around me, tucking it tight, rubbing my arms.

"You must get warm, Charlotte," he says. His face is close to mine. The night is in his eyes. He smells of smoke and embers and cloves. I want to rest against him. I want to be in his arms again. I am tight in blankets. "You have had a fright." He stands and moves to a corner where the moon doesn't follow him. His shape is almost lost. I hear liquid pouring. A bitter smell. And then he holds a tumbler of whisky to me. "Drink, Charlotte. It will warm you while I make a fire." I wriggle an arm free and reach for the glass. My fingers touch his. Then the cool glass is in my shaking hand. I sip the whisky – it heats my throat and belly. He crouches at the cold fireplace. There is urgency in his shoulders. I hear the rustle of kindling, and then the strike of iron on flint. Sparks. A flame. He arranges the logs, leans back. Small flames grow and the room golds. I find I am holding an empty glass. I am unsure how to ask for more. He takes the glass to the corner of the room. I can watch him there now the fire has filled it with rosy light. He pours the whisky and brings it to me. "Are you feeling better?" he asks. His face is affettuoso. I try to tell him yes, but my voice is a tripping thing. I sip. The whisky is smoothing me out and I feel it in my limbs. "Curse that wretched tradition. I've always hated it. My mother, you see," he says. But I do not.

"I thought all women were to wear white dresses," I say. I am nearing the end of the glass and a sleepiness is in my toes.

"Do you mean to tell me that you were not intending to be the White Lady?" There is so much listening in his face. How close he is. His eyes have gold in them. I hear the music of him – G Minor – con brio. He takes the empty glass from me and sets it on the table. "Charlotte."

"Drellop told me it was tradition to wear white." My only dress from home. I can feel the mud on the hem. I had wanted him to see me.

"Drellop had you wear a white dress?" There's a darkness in his voice – he is angry, but not with me. He stands above me, and the rosy light goes into the lines that have appeared on his forehead. "Did she tell you it is our tradition to have someone play the White Lady? And that person is carried to that wretched horse?" I am so smoothed out that understanding takes a long time to start in me. Drellop invited me and told me to wear this dress and forced my cloak from me and laughed at me behind her witch face. How afeared I was. Malicious creature. I am filled all the way with anger. It takes my tongue so that

I can only shake my head at him. A quick intake of breath. His hands clench. Then he sits by me on the sofa. I feel the weight of him. "Charlotte, you would not have been harmed. Whoever plays the White Lady is only taken to the horse to be sung to. Though I am certain the song would have injured your musical sensibilities." He smiles at me though I am not ready for amusement, and he realises for the smile is dropped and my hand is taken in his. I do not want him to let go. The rose glow and the voice of the fire and the night in the window behind us have begun to feel like dream stuff, soft and vanishing. I do not know if this is sleeping or waking. "I would not have allowed you to be harmed, Charlotte."

Chapter Nine

The moon is thin, the stars are still,
The White Lady walks on Dragon Hill,
She calls me once, she calls me twice,
Her voice touches me like ice,
The wind is her stallion, she rides it near,
The tap at my window tells me she's here.
I pull back my curtain, I see her face,
Pearl skin, pearl hair, her dress white lace.
'Come with me child, come with me now,
The beast of Koyn is on the prowl.
The hill is open, he climbs the night,
The stars tremble and shake in fright.
He will hunt and he will slay,
Those who cower, quake, and pray.
But keep by my side, hold my hand,
And come with me to my homeland.'

Did Prudence write this to taunt me? Her countenance is all innocence – she reads without a glance upwards - she turns the pages tranquillo. No smirk dances at the edges of her mouth. She does not let her hair fall over her face. Her penmanship is smooth. But perhaps she has just had a gifted teacher? For Drellop was all sincerity when the master had her apologise to me: her words were toothless, and she laid a gentle hand on my arm. It was only in the spring of her step that I heard her triumph. For she walked in three four time down the corridors, and the stairway, and the halls until I could no longer hear her. Heels can laugh.

"Have you read my composition, Miss Chant?" Her voice tiptoes, but her gaze strides. She is seeking my discomfort, trying to read it in my brow or my posture.

"Your lines differ in meter, Prudence. I believe you could do better." I smile adagio. Her weasel face studies mine. Her hands are folded on her desk. Her thin fingers are clasped – I fear them pointing at me. For I have seen her at a window when I walk with him, and I do not tell him she watches us. Not when we pause to see the kestrel hover and dive. Nor when we wish on falling leaves. Three weeks since All Hallows Eve, and I know not dates, but mist pooling in field corners, dawn lighting the hilltops, and his step in the golden woods. He has not taken my hand again, yet his fingers brushed mine when we stood fog deep in a vanishing world. And sometimes we are so close, I think he can hear the music. And what music shimmering in the wind! We chased it, though he said he only wanted to keep pace with me. And afterwards, I played it to him until the fortepiano ached in protest. 'You play loud enough to wake the White Horse,' he said, and he lit candles as the sunset thinned.

There's a pang in me and I turn to the window – a floating white land faces me. I can only see the hills faintly in the fog, and fainter still as I linger. The White Horse lays in a landscape as pale as itself. I shiver. I can't help but remember Wellack's story of the White Lady and her 'elsewhere' with a sun that waxed and waned like the moon.

"Papa's not riding in the fog, Miss Chant. He returned before this lesson," Prudence says. I startle. She is beside me, peering out the window.

"I wasn't looking for him." Though I speak too swiftly.

"Papa knows not to ride in a fog when she's walking." She presses her hands to the pane and her breath mists the glass. It is as if the fog is inside her. I want to inch away.

"We have thirty minutes left – you need to work on your poem. Back to your desk, Prudence." But she does not move. Her pointy chin is all stubbornness.

"Has he warned you about the fog? When the hills disappear, that's when she's here." She takes her hands off the window, leaving prints on the glass, and looks at me with her weasel eyes. I itch to move away from her.

"That sounds like the beginning of another verse. You had better write it down before you forget it." I walk to her desk and pull the chair out with a clatter. I set the poem down, and find I am thankful to no longer hold it. "Sit, Prudence." But she does not. She stands framed by the fog. Her copper hair is startling against the white and is echoed in the freckles across her nose. She looks at me with pickled loathing.

"He didn't warn you, did he?" She lifts her pointy chin. How am I to answer without revealing myself? And what need is there – she has seen us in the mist. Ought he to have warned me? In the fog, we only met music, bittersweet and soaring. There was no White Lady, there was only us. I remember his fingers brushing mine and my pulse quickens. "He didn't, did he?"

"Prudence, this tale you're telling, you ought to write it down." I tap her desk. "What an imagination you have! Have you been reading novels?" But my voice wobbles. I want to close the curtains on the white windows. She tilts her head as if listening to faraway and her eyes widen. There's a pause that feels like chasing.

"Can you hear her?" she says. Her face is all wonder and gasp. She turns and peers, raising up on her toes to try for a better view, though there is nothing to obstruct it.

"There's no one there, Prudence. Enough of this nonsense." But I can't help and look past her into the white, into the floating world, into the silence now turning to song. A melody in D Minor pierces me and pulls me to the window. Is this the music of the fog? A longing begins in me – to be in that vanished world and feel it chill on my dress. If I followed the music, would it lead me to that elsewhere where the fog crystals under a sickle sun?

"You look like one of the mice the kitchen cat brings in, Miss," Prudence laughs. There is a hunting feeling in the air. And a coldness that creeps up my arms. I wrap my shawl tighter around my shoulders. "Why are you so afeared? It is only the White Lady. The beast of Koyn hasn't woken." Her gaze pinches me.

"The beast is your own invention, Prudence. You wrote of it this very lesson." Wellack made no mention of a creature in the hill. Nor was there any pantomime of a beast on All Hallows Eve. Though I shudder to remember the bull man carrying me into the dark and the masks following, crowding, chanting.

"He's sleeping in the hill. You won't see him, yet." She taps a rhythm on the window with her thin fingers. Two minims followed by triplets. "I put my ear to the hill and tried to hear him, but Papa became angry with me. He was afeared."

"I expect your father was just tired of your nonsense," I say, but a memory stirs me. The smell of chalk, the taste of gingerbread, the prickle of grass through my dress. A dare. Steps down the slope. And I was alone, so alone. From the White Horse's eye, I saw the sun set in the north and strange stars come and I felt – I felt a beating in the ground. How like a heartbeat it was. How it thrummed through me and welded me to that spot. Was it the beast sleeping under the chalk?

"If you believe it's nonsense, why don't you climb the hill?" Prudence says. "My mama would go out in these fogs. She said the White Lady would never harm her. She said her family came from the

White Lady's daughter." There's a waver in her voice. Pity fills my sails. Poor motherless child. She pretends the White Lady haunts Moorvale so she can think her mother was not mad. Or perhaps it's a way to be close to her? There's a tug at my heart. After Pa Mountberry died, I rode his chestnut mare, Bramble, terror-fast through the lavender fields and made the world a blur of purple and tears.

"Prudence, there's no one there." I lay a moth-light hand on her arm, and she does not shrug me off. "Perhaps you would like to read for the rest of your lesson."

"Papa doesn't allow me in the library now, and I've read all my books so many times, I know them by heart." Her voice is small. Her eyes lowered. If she were permitted to her mother's library, perhaps she would have no need for these fancies? I find I am frustrated with him. How could he deny his daughter the meagre comfort of her mother's books?

"You must be allowed to read. I will talk to him," I say. Her eyes meet mine and I nod a promise. For I will battle to bring something of her mother back to her, though paper and print are not a smile or a touch. How better to seek her mother in books well read and beloved, than in the delirium that hollowed her? There is an ache in my chest. What do I have of my Ma? Where are her poppy fields? The sun rose and set in those hedgerows. The stars were carried on that wind. I turn back to the windows, to hide the tears in my eyes. The world is white, white, white. I hear Prudence sit at her desk and turn the dry pages of her book. I glance over my shoulder at her – there is hope on her brow. I will not let her down. I will help her. And he will listen to me. I turn back to the fog, and I do not strain for an outline, for the hills. I let the floating world soothe me. And music largo, as largo as the sleep of whales rises. Then I see. I see – a figure. Someone is there. Moving slowly through the fog as though it were a tide. My breath catches. I peer. They are made up of graceful lines that disappear and reappear as the fog shifts. And with each vanishing, I feel they are my fancy. For who would venture into that world? My heart is quavers, but I keep my breathing steady. Steady so Prudence does not look up from her book. I hear her turning another page. I press my hands to the window. The glass is chill and damp. There the figure is again. Not so far away. Not on the path but walking the wet lawn. The music in me turns grave and the fog shifts again. And I see her. A woman. A woman in a white dress. I snatch my hands from the window. I leave prints – they drip. Her hair is black and rich like night boiled in a cauldron. Her figure is tall and stately. The fog moves again, hiding her. I see only the dark of her hair. I hear myself swallowing. Who is she? There was no bracing against the cold in her posture: she walked as if it didn't touch her, though she must be chilled to her core. The fog thins. She has halted. She is standing still. The fog tucks into her hair, into her dress. There's a listening in her. But I did not call her. I did not call her. Dread pierces me. I do not want her to turn. I do not want to see her face. Does she know I'm watching her? I cannot pull away from the window. The fog wafts. I see the outline of the hills behind her. I will her to walk on and not look back. I grip the ledge. She is turning. She is turning. Her face. Her beautiful face. It is her. His wife. She sees me. She sees me. Fog on fog. It thickens. It cloaks. I cannot see her. The fog moves again. It drains. Sunlight sifts. The hills come. But she is gone.

Chapter Ten

I dream of fire in a white stone. And a ring cold on my finger. Sunset in the north and the hill at my back. I breathe dying light. And I am not alone. Though I know the others only as hands leading me up. Up the hill. The wind is with me. My dress is white. I do not look at my way. I look at my hem – long and trailing. At my feet – bare and chill. Someone says my name. But they are in the dark. I hold my hands to the strange stars. And the fire in the stone gilds the night.

Then I wake - my heart quavers. And I scramble to my little window to pull back the grey curtain, for the stars, for the sun rising in the East. There's frost and dawn on the glass, and I trace silver with my fingers. The wings of winter are over the hills, and the clouds wait, heavy with snow. My breath is puffs. A red fox runs. And I hear a sparkling melody, light as snowflakes in a dove wind. G Major – spiritoso. How it lifts me. How it makes me feel I could have feathers. If only I was a girl again seeking the silver owl. 'The silver owl brings winter when she wakes. Where she flies, the fields go thorny with frost and the clouds go fat with snow.' Ma pointed to icicles and said the owl rested in those trees. And years after, Emmie and I searched for silver feathers until we were called in for blankets and firesides and steaming pies. There's a pang in my heart. Winter is in Elderford. In the willow brook and the south field. How many weeks since Emmie's letter? Yet, I have written to her over and over. Perhaps her plan to save Oricala failed? Perhaps Oricala was never delivered to Arunspear? Lady Mountberry spoke of an axe. Would she…? Is my Oricala firewood? My hands tremble, so I rest them on the window, but a sob still comes. The kingdom Pa Mountberry gave me – is it ash? I am in another kingdom now, and it is not mine.

Christmas is a creeping thing at Moorvale. It has no crown or trumpets or dancing step. It makes itself small. Small enough to fit in glimpses and corners – a sprig of holly, a clump of ivy, a whiff of nutmeg. How vast Christmas was at Elderford. So vast it made a land of every room and a day of every moment. We breathed spice and merriment, we laughed with full bellies, and we sang till the candles trembled. We looked through Pa Mountberry's telescope for the Bethlehem star. Emmie said she saw it over the south field. Lady Mountberry sent us to bed before the mummers came, and we sang 'while shepherds watched their flock by night' to keep from falling asleep. Later, we sneaked to the top of the great staircase, and held hands through ticking minutes tall as centuries, my eyelids drooping, the cold at my toes, and Emmie whispering she heard steps on the drive. But at the first knock on the front door, we fled.

I walk the corridors. Morning seeps through the windows, reluctant to tend to Moorvale. I clutch my sheet music, my gift for him. Four carols - robins plucking berries and frost jewels on the lawn, sunset caught in icicles and snow falling on a sickle moon. I have walked winter alone. He has not been beside me in the silver woods or the white winds. He has shut himself in her library, in her forbidden rooms. He has not called me Charlotte since I spoke to him of Prudence, though he hesitates at 'Miss Chant.' I am nameless now. I am glad Prudence has the solace of her mother's books. But must she leave them open on her desk? For I cannot help but read the inscriptions. The raven and his bride. My loneliness is so large I feel it cannot fit inside me. How many times did it have to fold itself in half? I halt at his study. I push the sheet music under the door. Will he greet me tonight at church, or will he look away?

I tie a green ribbon in my hair. It is my only festivity, for Christmas has not visited my grey room. The snow has stopped falling and now the fields sleep under the moon. The stars are low and tumbling on the hills. The night is a carol. Suddenly, there's a knock on my door. I do not want to turn from my window. The knock comes again. Louder.

"Charlotte, are you there? Charlotte?" It is him. I pull the door open. "Have you seen her?" There is panic on his brow. He grips the door frame. I want to reach for his hand and take it in mine.

"Who?" I ask.

"Prudence. She's nowhere to be found. She wouldn't miss church – she was always ready and waiting by the door at least half an hour before we had to leave. And we are due to leave in five minutes." I want to take him into my room and sit him on my meagre chair, but I do not.

"Then there are still five minutes. I suspect she is lost within the pages of a novel. And Moorvale is so vast, how many perfect nooks for reading…"

"Drellop has had the maids search the house thrice over." His eyes are wide with worry. I find my hand is on his arm – I snatch it away.

"Did they look everywhere? When I was a girl, I had enough hiding places to fill a map."

"That's why I hoped you might – you've been closer to her since…" He cannot bring himself to speak of his bride's books. His eyes flash appassionato. Envy pinches me, so I look at the floor, at the rug's fraying edge. "Charlotte, did she tell you anything?"

"Anything?" His hand is on my wrist. It jolts through me. But what can I say? For Prudence has told me nothing of her secrets or hiding places, she talks only of her mother. There's an ache in me for poppy fields and dandelion time. I glance upwards. "Have you looked in Lady Selwyn's rooms?"

"That wing is kept locked." His eyes scald me.

"Prudence is clever. If she were so inclined, she could enter without you noticing."

"Through a locked door?"

"Behind you if it is only locked when you leave." His eyes are cooling. "If I had had a place to be close to my mother…" He takes my hand in his. He grips it firmly. I am half floating half hesitating. But I do not want him to let go. Our fingers are entwining. I hear a thunder in D Minor. Then he is pulling me towards the door, and we are along the corridors, so fast, my feet are triplets to his crotchets. Moorvale is a blur of dark wood and deeper shadows, of candles battling night and Christmas hinting in holly. And then we are at a closed door, and he is letting go of my hand and producing a weighty key. I look away. There's a click and then the creak of hinges. And there is the scent of snow and hill - a chill gust from an open window.

"Charlotte." He is framed in the doorway, a candlestick in his hand. The flames bend and dance. The shadows on his face mimic his devil's mask. He wants me to follow him into the darkness that feels like trespassing, and I do not want to go with him. I have seen her in mist and mirror. I do not want to see her in the dark. "Help me, Charlotte." There is pleading in his eyes, and an ache answers in me. I find my fingers touching his outstretched hand. I cannot turn from him. Though the music I hear is furioso – chords descending and descending – so low they quake. His hand grips my fingers and then I am by his side, his arm pressed against mine. I feel the warmth of him. I breathe his scent of oaks and hearths. We step through the doorway. My heartbeat is forte. He holds the candle stick high, and the light goes ahead of us, slowly touching the portraits on the walls. Faces look at us, and there is warning in their eyes. We do not walk quickly, but there is so much running in me. He grips my hand harder. We pause by tables, by sideboards, by deep windows, and the candle glow goes into hollows and hiding places. But Prudence is not there. The night feels like watching. Another doorway passes over us. The scent of lavender. I hear something – a soft step – silk skirts.

"Prudence?" My voice tumbles through the gloom. He squeezes my hand. We wait in the silence. Nothing. He lets go of me and sets the candle stick on a table. Then I see – wood carved with faces of leaf and grimace, framing velvet in deep reds: a four-poster bed. We are in her room. My breath catches – the raven and his bride. There is a twist inside me. How I want to flee. But I would not find my way.

"Where is she, Charlotte?" There is so much worry in his face. I want to touch him, his brow, but her room watches me. I am heavy with shame, so I look from him. Then I see a book lying open on the bed. I lift it carefully so that my fingers don't brush the velvet, and I bring it to the meagre light. It is heavy in my hands, so I lay it on the table, and I read:

She cut her thumb on the frost thorne and the ice was sleep, and the sleep was a sea. And ice, like vines, grew round her. Her breath was dreams. Her face a ghost. And only then did the beast of Koyn lay down its head and close its eyes.

"The beast of Koyn! I thought it was Prudence's invention. She wrote of it in a lesson," I say. "She was here. This proves it." He sweeps the book up, and I reach to point out the passage, but he slams it shut, almost catching my fingers. There is agitation on his forehead. His face is as closed as the tome he is clutching to his chest. "She was here." But he does not listen to me. Did he give his bride this book when they were young? Did he read to her under the oaks? Have I tainted it with my touch? Humiliation stings me, so I stride to the curtains, pushing the weighty velvet aside, for the window, for a sight that isn't the Lady Selwyn's book or bed or husband. The night is snow and moon and prayers. The hills sparkle in time with the stars. The cold breathes over me. I shiver. There is such stillness in the slopes and the fields, in the woods without wind. A stillness that beckons you to lie down in it. Where are you, Prudence? There is a shining emptiness. And then a wisp of an E Minor melody nudges me, coaxes me, calls me. Calls me on and up and high. The hills. The hills. An understanding shakes me. I turn and meet his bleak gaze. "Prudence has gone to the White Horse," I say.

Chapter Eleven

There is a moment like a quaver stretching into a semibreve, a moment that makes me wonder if I have spoken at all. His eyes widen, and I hear the book drop to the floor. Then he is panic and footsteps and a shape I am following through the dark, the dark that clutches and misleads me. I am buffeted by wood and wall and corner. I lose sight of him. He calls me and I follow his voice. And I feel half underground, half ghost, until finally, I see a doorway of candlelight and silhouette. He grips my hand, and we are running and fear and clamour. At the top of the great stairway, he lets go and starts down without me, taking the steps two at a time, three at a time. I rush behind him. Drellop looks up at us, her face stewed worry. Servants stand in whispering groups.

"You didn't find Prudence?" Drellop asks. I am surprised at the feeling in her voice.

"She's gone to the White Horse. I am certain of it."

"But it's been hours since anyone saw her. She…" Her words hang, and the silence that follows is made of the cold that beats at the windows, the pale faces that watch, and a fear like fangs.

"There's no need for alarm. Prudence has her mother's constitution. A bit of snow cannot do her much harm." He speaks in G Major, his countenance pride, but he summons Drellop near and I hear his low words. "Send for the doctor." He looks at me. "Miss Chant."

And then I am with him, in stride and purpose, my steps in time with his. Drellop's stare prickles my back until we round the corner out of her sight. He leans like tumbling against the wall.

"Charlotte, I…" And he says no more, but I meet him in the unspoken. And when he lifts his head, I am with him, I am with him. His hands in my hands. His pulse in my pulse. Then he is upright and resolve and fast and we are a hurry in the corridors. We bundle into boots, and he wraps my cloak around my shoulders, his fingers brushing my neck. The air is urgency and clamour, but we don't wait for the men. I take a lantern. The door swings wide. And then we are plunged into the night. A star shatter night. That's what Ma called them because 'even the stars are going to freeze and crack into bits, and we'll be picking the shards out the fields for a week.'

My heart pangs. My breath puffs. All is ice and bright. The moon flashes white on the hills. The sky is bitter with stars. The snow is unmarked by fox or robin or foot. It is like a taunt. I want to dent it, ruin its serenity.

"There are no footsteps," he says. "Yet, it stopped snowing hours ago. Prudence has been out in it all that time. Why? What if she's fallen on the hill? She... Why didn't I notice earlier that she was gone?" I grip his arm, but I cannot soothe with words for I have thought him a neglectful father. I have compared him to Pa Mountberry. For he does not teach Prudence planets or scales. And he leaves her alone in the valley of her grief. And now he sees himself, too. There is guilt in his shoulders. Then guilt in his stride. He kicks the snow into flurries. He is a dark shape amongst white. A shape growing smaller. I run to him.

We walk in the stinging cold. How it fights us. How it holds us back. How it commands we surrender. There's snow deep on my skirts, on my cloak. It hits my legs. Ice in my boots. My feet hurt. My breathing smarts. I pause to look at the men who follow – dark and hurrying and lanterns swinging. The cold furies through me. It demands I stop. But he is still onwards and onwards. Does he notice I am gone? He turns, looks over his shoulder. My name. Shame blooms in me. I run as I can, though I cannot feel my feet or ankles. He waits for me. We go on. The cold is thickening, thickening through the fields, through the sky. Then we are at the hill.

There is no White Horse long and startle bright. No great eye watches the night. I hear a melody sour and shivering – doloroso. Does it come from the horse under the snow? A begging tune. An outstretched hand of a tune. It takes me. I am walking in it, wading in it. I am heart deep in it. It has taken my hand and I have taken his. On and on. I hardly feel. I am bone cold, soul cold. On and on. We are high. We are with the moon. And when I look back, I see fields, patchworks of white, such a long way to where the stars dip down to meet them. It dizzies me. There is so much stillness. Does it hold Prudence? Did it coax her to lie down?

We are where the horse is hidden. We are here. There is so much falling here – so steep, so high. He is ahead. I stumble. I have not his sureness of foot. He is shouting. He is shouting. And I go swiftly as I can – like a sparrow in a damning gale. I do not know how I get to him without slipping into the vale, but then I am. And there lies Prudence. She could be sleeping. Her weasel hair fans out. Her countenance is dreams. There's no hint of injury in her limbs – no twisting, no red marking the snow. She had wrapped her cloak about her. She had chosen to lie in the cold. Because of the stillness? And now there's a spinning in the night in the air in me. I am crouching. I am scrambling for her wrist. I feel. I feel her pulse. My face is wet. Relief bursts in me. He weeps. He crouches and gathers her into his arms. Snow dusts her. Snow is all over him. Gently, so gently, he lifts her. I take off my cloak, shake it, and pull off the crusts of ice. And then I drape it over her. The night rattles through me. We turn. We are going home – where the lights lead. Me ahead. I'm running. I am awake, awake, awake. I shout at the men. I wave my arms. I run and I run until I do not know how I am at the bottom of the hill. When I turn, I see him carrying her. I have left my lantern on the hill. I see the shine of it. A piddly star. The men are all around. Thundering.

Lanterns swinging. They pass me like rain. And I run on. And on. I do not know how I am so fast. I do not feel. I only go.

I am at Moorvale. I am under its gloomy heights, its black windows. I'm beating my fist on the door. I'm shouting so loudly my throat hurts. The door opens. Drellop. But not a Drellop I have met. For this one takes my frozen hands in hers. This one has thankfulness in her face. This one brings me inside the warmth. This one snaps her fingers at a maid who wraps me in a blanket. This one leads me to a fireplace. Heat washes me. My legs give way. I am caught by hands and ushered into a deep chair.

"Drink," Drellop says as a maid pushes a glass into my shaking hand. The smell tingles my nose. I struggle to hold the glass. I can barely bring it to my lips. I sip. Fire down my throat. Someone is unlacing my boots, pulling them off. I can't wriggle my toes.

"Prudence… how long till the doctor comes?" I ask.

"We expect him soon." But there is waiting and watching and pacing in her voice. I gulp the rest of the whisky and its burning shudders through me. My feet are thawing. Clamour. I hear Caleb – his voice – low as if not to disturb his daughter. Clamour. Many steps.

The men are with him. Boots down the corridors. Boots up the stairways. I must go to him. I raise myself from the chair. I'm a wobbling thing.

"Miss Chant, you need to rest," Drellop says. But I go on – my thawing feet hurt – my hem sheds ice.

Chapter Twelve

There is so little climbing left in me. I can barely take the stairs. The banister is smooth under my hand. Lamplight wipes the walls, turning everything sleepy. I am bone tired - soul tired. Along the corridors, towards his voice, I am pulled. I must be chill in my snow melt dress, but I don't feel. His voice. His voice. I am in the doorway. Heat blazes from the room, rushing around me, passing me like I am a rock in a stream. I am untouched by it. Prudence still sleeps. Her face is peacefulness. But the maids are working at warming her, waking her. Blankets and fire and her father who clutches her hand. How gently he speaks to her. How he smooths her hair. How handsome I thought him before, but now – he is all tenderness. He is beautiful. And fear ices through me. What if she doesn't wake? What if the doctor cannot bring her back to him? My eyes prick. Then he glances up, sees me. And before I can blink away my tears, he is clutching me tightly, so tightly. I am all floating and worry. And I do not want him to let go.

"Charlotte, how did you know? If it wasn't for you, she... I would've lost her." He loosens his grip. Then his hands are smoothing my hair, running down my arms, entwining with my fingers. "You're freezing. Your dress is soaked."

"It was just a bit of ice. And it melted." But there's shiver in my smile. His hands move up my arms. There is even more shiver in me when he touches me. Then he pulls me against him as if to warm me with himself. And how warm he is. As if spared by the bitter night. Though he still smells of the sky on the hills. His hands rub my freezing back. I tremble. I am all collapse and sigh. I cannot help but lean into him. Over his shoulder, I watch Prudence. I will her eyelids to quiver and open. Yet still she sleeps. But the maids are no longer fussing her, they are staring at me and the master. Their hands are slack and there's scandal in their gawping mouths. It smacks me. I pull away from him, though all in me aches as I am cold once more.

"You'll catch your death if you don't change out of those sodden things."

"I'm staying with you. There's no need to worry about me. Prudence…" I whisper. The gaze of the maids is a chastisement.

"You must. Or you will catch a chill. And I cannot have the doctor distracted by a second patient." He tries a smile. "And besides, being properly attired is a necessity of your position and that means – no dresses that drip snowmelt along my corridors."

"Very well then, sir," I nod. And that look in his eyes warms my way through the hallways and the stairways. I am thankful to find a fire in my room. Bronze glow glides. I do not allow myself to sit, for I could not bring myself to stand. The meagre chair, the narrow bed – they beckon me to rest. But I am out of my freezing clothes as swiftly as my stiff fingers can manage. And when I am changed, I don't linger.

There's another voice drifting from Prudence's room. A bassoon of a voice. Largo. Too low for me to catch the words. But his tone is D Major – hope. From the doorway, I see the doctor, all wiriness and whiskers, and Caleb, heads together. There's gratefulness in Caleb's nod and in the unclenching of his hands. I let the doorframe prop me up. I let the blazing heat go through me. My heartbeat fills me. Prudence has colour in her cheeks, meagre colour – a pink dawn passing a snowdrop. Her hands are still limp, but no longer deathly white. Caleb turns and beckons me.

"Miss Chant, Prudence's governess," he introduces me. The doctor looks at me like a king to a dormouse. I meet his disdain with a lion glare. "Doctor Bradley, if it wasn't for Miss Chant, I would never have found my daughter in time. It was she... I had no idea. I have not been the father that I ought to have been. And it has nearly cost me Prudence. But now – everything will change. Everything." And with that, he takes my hand and raises it to his lips. I do not feel my feet. I am not inside myself. Music is fizzing, golden, about us. I hear myself laughing. But it seems to come from elsewhere. Then my hand is tight in his. The warmth of him. I am pressed to his side. I am more than thawed. I do not think I have ever been so warm. I am basking, I am melting, I am burning. "I did not introduce you properly before, Doctor Bradley. This is Charlotte." My name giddies me. The doctor has horror in his whiskery eyebrows, in his walrus glare. If he is not careful, his eyebrows will waggle off his face and careen down the corridors. More laughter, and it is me again. The doctor packs his bag. It clicks shut. He pulls on his coat.

"Well, Lord Selwyn, I must depart. When your daughter wakes, confine her to her bed for a week. She could still develop a cold. She must be kept warm and well fed." His eyes graze me, measure me, condemn me. Does he compare me to Faith? She was grandeur and mystery. A prayer uttered in a temple on the moon. The music wilts as I glimpse myself in the mirror. And I? I am a conversation between a hedgerow and a puddle. There's a sinking in me. I feel the floor. I feel my own weight. I let go of Caleb's hand. The doctor nods and is gone. And though he walks in 2/4 time, his footsteps sound like mockery.

Then Caleb is holding me again. My name. My name. All is shining, all is stars. He hushes, he strokes my hair, my temple. It shivers me.

"Caleb, I..."

"Everything will be different now, Charlotte. Everything." He is leaning towards me. His hand cups my chin. I close my eyes. Then suddenly, we are not alone.

"Papa." Prudence is awake. And he is kneeling by her bed, he is all tears. And she is weeping, too. Great sobs move her weary frame. Her face reddens. I rush to the table, pour a glass of water from the jug, and offer it to her. She does not shake her head, but the loathing in her eyes makes me scurry, glass in hand, to the doorway. He smooths the tear-soaked hair from her face.

"Prudence… why did you?" His voice is half whisper, half scolding.

"I didn't mean to.... The cold made me sleepy."

"What possessed you to go there? You're not a daft girl, Prudence. You know not to dally on the hills in these temperatures. What would have become of you if Char… if Miss Chant…" There it is – Miss Chant – the governess. I cannot swallow the lump in my throat. And though Prudence is too weak to lift her head, she scowls.

"Miss Chant. It's always Miss Chant."

"What are you talking about?" Though there is guilt in how he turns his face from her, how he does not glance in my direction. A glacier of dread has begun to move in me, slowly, until I am frozen through. He denied me. My hand trembles on the glass.

"I've seen you with her. You don't notice me watching because you don't notice me at all." Her face is red as fury. "I wanted to be with Mama again. On the White Horse like we used to be. When it was just us. You didn't come with us, and we didn't need you." She rolls on her side, wracking with her sobs. He rests a gentle hand on her shoulder, but she shrugs it off.

"Prudence, I know I haven't been a good father to you. I have thought only of myself. I've wallowed in my grief. But if you let me… we can be a family once more." Her sobs slow. She looks over her shoulder at him. "Prudence, you are my only child, and I would do anything to win you back to me."

"Anything?" A glint in her worn eyes. A glint I do not welcome. She is trying to prop herself up on her pillows. She flops down. There is victory in how she rests, hair tangled, face flushed. I gulp the water to stop my hand shaking on the glass. The heat stifles.

"Anything, Prudence." He is all softness.

"Send Miss Chant away," she shouts into sobs. He jolts. The air tilts and squeezes. My heart flails. I want to wrap my arms round him, dig my fingers into his collar and not let go, not let him banish me. Am I breathing as he sinks his head into his hands? Am I breathing as he scrapes his fingers through his dark hair? I did not know until now how much I wanted him to be my home.

"I cannot." The words strangle out of him. And the need in them presses the glacier from me. A sob is building in me. I struggle to keep it in. Eyes on me. Hateful eyes.

"But you promised."

"You don't understand, Prudence. Without her… without her… I cannot."

"Send her away, Papa." A fury of pleading. Her hands in fists. I inch from her sight over to the shadowed corner of the room. The walls cushion me.

"Prudence. I need her. We need her." His voice is quietness and urging. "If she leaves…" He shakes his head. "We can't let her." And there's something in his words that baffles me. His tone has turned like a falcon in the currents. And the currents are pulling me, too. He has stood. He is beckoning me. I cannot help but drift as if my feet are not my own. I am at his side. His arm presses against me. It props me up, keeps me from falling. "We will be a family again, Prudence. Thanks to Charlotte. Charlotte will make us a family once more." There is conquering in his smile. Rapids of joy sweep me. I am with him, and he is my home.

Chapter Thirteen

"Are you going to play for me, Miss Chant?" Prudence says, her tone stinging syrup. I look over my shoulder from where I sit on the piano stool. She is a bundle of blankets and spite. "Papa says you wish to entertain me." She lowers herself on the chair by the window, rests her chin on her palm, and wafts 'proceed' with her other hand. My fingers jitter. I want to win her. For myself and for him. But the melody she prompts is a sly thing of creeping and plotting. I face the keyboard.

"If your father thinks it's appropriate for you to be out of bed when your week of rest is not yet up, I am happy to amuse you, Prudence. This is a song I wrote when I was years younger than you are now. I called it 'Marion and the Pirate King.'" Opening notes. Wistfulness winds into warning. I take a breath and sing.

> *There was a lady lived in the wind,*
> *She flew over hill, wood, valley, and sea,*
> *Saw a pirate king, oh black eyed was he,*
> *And she wished so hard she sinned.*
> *They called him Robert the Raven,*
> *The seven seas were under his whip,*
> *The Kraken's Eye was a fearsome ship,*

For evil men it was a haven.
Its sails were black and billowing,
Its prow could slice the moon from the sky,
Its flag was five rays from a black eye,
And at the wheel was the pirate king.

From the wind, Marion called to him,
But he only heard the waves and gale,
His men's shanties and song of a whale,
His face handsome and grim.
Marion was neither ghost nor wraith,
But a lady in the cradle cursed,
For her last step to be her first,
Her cloak of five winds kept her safe.
She had no kin but falcons and rains,
Her bed sunset, her fireplace dawn,
Her face by storm and sorrow was worn,
No pathway home, only the star lanes.

Her roads were hail bursts and lightning
Her cloak of five winds whipped the sky
Along the trail of The Kraken's Eye
She saw seven seas under death's wing
Robert Raven, black of eye and heart
His Kingdom battle, his crown treasure
His victims lost, their cries his pleasure.
Yet Marion could not from him part
Though she saw ships break and sink and bleed
Though his cannons made a fire of night
Though his name did summon dread and fright
To be near him was her breath and need.

When she saw an armada fierce
She knew the swift ships carried his doom
His home, the sea would become his tomb
For his cannons could never pierce
The armada that followed arrow fast,

Its treasure his judgement and his end.
Marion could not his torn sails mend,
So tied her cloak of winds to the mast,
And fell into the waves and drowned.
Without a word or glance from he
She sank to the graveyard in the sea
Never remembered and never found.

Now, Robert and his men sail the sky
Listen, his cannons are the thunder
Quake, it's his ship you are under,
Pray and hide from The Kraken's Eye.

The final chord. And then sturdy applause. I spin. Caleb is clapping. He strides past Prudence, sweeps me from the stool, gathers me in his arms. But my song is still inside me and something echoes – for I saw raven in him. And he feels raven now when his arms are black wings around me, when my name is dark in his voice. A shudder moves me. And I remember Ma's warning 'never feed a raven for it may be the cruel king who was cursed and is always in the night and always hungry and hunting. Any maiden that feeds him becomes his winged bride.' And then I remember the master's bride in the fog – her beautiful face, her accusing eyes. Was she my fancy? I used to dream of Crenacal of the bogs, the lady whose lantern is a wisp, who only shows her true face, her crone face, to those she drowns. And once I thought I saw her where the stream becomes rocks and tumble and mist. For a white lady reached ghostly for me, and I ran weeping home.

"Prudence," I say, pulling away from him. His daughter is pickled loathing. There is so much fury in her small frame, I am surprised she can fit it all inside her without bursting at the seams.

"It's time for you to return to your bed rest, Prudence," he says.

"But, Papa, I'm half dead with boredom."

"And you were nearly entirely dead, Prudence. If it wasn't for…"

"Yes, yes. Miss Chant."

"Charlotte. It would be well for you to accustom yourself with her name." And with that, she half flounces, half shuffles from the room. Her steps are soft and vanishing. His hand is on my arm. "She'll come round."

"How can you be so certain?" I move to the window and the white scene greets me as if it has no memory. The bare trees do not hold that yesterday in their branches. There are only robins, merry and round. And there is no terror or searching in the smooth snow or the cloud sky. No wind to summon flurries. His hands are on my shoulders. I feel his touch all through me. I lean against him.

"Prudence has made a confession to me. One that I must pass on to you, Charlotte, though I beg you not to think ill of her. The blame for her behaviour lies with me - my neglect of her."

"What confession?" I turn, and his face is all earnestness and frowns.

"Prudence told me that she had deliberately frightened you. That you believed her tales of the White Lady and the Beast of Koyn."

"I did not believe her. And I told her as such." Yet I cannot meet his gaze. I turn back to the window, and I watch the crows crossing the sky to its very edge. But indignation is uncurling in me. Cruel child. I had tried to help her. My eyes are pricking. She will never like me. She will never want me here. I will fail. I am a child again in the yew shadows, craving a kind word from Lady Mountberry. I see her chestnut curls bobbing, how gently she strokes Emmie's dark hair – its gloss, its sheen. My plait in my hand is straw. A pang.

"Charlotte." His voice wakes me, coaxes me.

"Yes, I was afeared. The fog. It… I thought I saw…but when the fog lifted there was nothing there. It was only my fancy. I was seeing things because, because…"

"Because of Prudence. Charlotte, I am sorry. You have my word of honour, there are no monsters here. Though if you wish, I shall have the maids check under every bed and in every cupboard." He smiles and my wound is washed clean.

"That would be unnecessary, though you may wish to check that Miss Drellop doesn't alter and transform into a beast should she eat wensleydale cheese during the witching hour. I believe I saw long claw marks in the cheese, yesterday. And the day before, I found a lengthy whisker in the butter."

"There are some who believe her to have fangs."

"Those she has bitten don't doubt her fangs." We laugh louder than jackdaws. I pull up my sleeve to display an imaginary bitemark, and he runs his thumb over my wrist. I am whirling once more.

"We should keep vigil at this window tonight." He turns me to face the white scene. "Perhaps we'll see her climb that oak right to the very top and try to claw the moon out of the sky. I trust that when you were taught the planets, you learned the moon is made of cheese."

"Of course, I was not so foolish that I mistook bitemarks for craters." We laugh, and it crackles through me, and shoos away frets and worries.

"Her mother filled her head with that wretched tale. It is just a tale, Charlotte. A cruel one. For it has taken so much. Don't let it take you from me, too."

"Just a tale," I mimic, but I am glad the window does not look upon the hills so that the memory of that other yesterday doesn't greet me. But still it creeps in me: gingerbread stuck to the roof of my mouth, Emmie laying in the grass, the dazzle of the horse made new again. And stepping onto its eye, and the sun, the sun. "She comes to those who see the sun setting in the north." I echo Wellack's words. Caleb's fingers tighten on my arms.

"I beg you not to listen to my poor daughter. Let us put everything behind us, Charlotte. I need you with me. And Prudence, well, she also needs you, despite her behaviour." And his voice is half commanding, half pleading. How he smells of hearths and winter.

How I long for him to be my home. But though I am all sighs and melt when he wraps his arms about me, still I see the sun setting in the north. A coldness beats into a melody, piercing and harsh, and suddenly his arms feel too heavy, too enclosing. "You will stay with me, won't you, Charlotte? We are only at the beginning." A warning in E Minor chills me. But then his hands are turning me to face him, are in my hair, are stroking my temple.

"Yes, Caleb, I'll stay with you." I say.

Chapter Fourteen

I dream of a beating in the ground. And the sky on my tongue. Sun passing over me and lowering in the north. And I cup the red sun in my palm. The ring on my finger is cold is white is fire. Then dark is over me. The strange stars come. They chill me in my white dress. I look at my hem. I am standing on the White Horse's eye. Chalk pieces hurt my feet. My voice sticks in me. My hands are limp. The moon is behind me. And I am not alone. Faces of horn and grin and fang and jeer. They are closing on me. They are closing on me.

I wake. I shake my dream from me. I do not turn it over in my hands to study it, I do not hold it to the window to see it better in the light. Instead, I shut it away and padlock it thrice. There will be no shadow clawing at this day. This day is a ballad. See how the spring is gentle on my curtains. See how the sky behind them is cornflowers. See how the blossom is a whisper on the trees. And we will walk in the woods where it tumbles pink and ivory and he will ask me… he will ask me. I have too much music in me, and it is the colour of those daffodils that are nodding in answer to the breeze. And it is the rhythm of those starlings swirling galaxies over the hills. I dare not play it out, dare not play it to Moorvale's envious walls and antique gloom, dare not have Drellop hear me. Though the old Drellop is quite gone. Gone is the mockery and scorn. For I have not encountered them since the night Prudence went to the White Horse, since the night we found her tomb-still in the snow. The new Drellop is respect and confidence and, would you believe, occasional humour. I am beginning to imagine her as a someday friend. It is as if she has finally taken off her witch mask.

A knock on my door. I open it a squirrel's inch for I am not yet dressed. Mary thrusts a letter at me. I do not blanche at her sour countenance, I take the letter greedily, and close the door. It has been months since Emmie's letter, though I have written whole realms to her. Her handwriting looks like sisterhood, like the dusks in the south field when the fawns treaded softly by, like the ribbons we tied in our hair for the balls. 'We will wear all the colours and leave none for anyone else,' Emmie laughed as Lady Mountberry disdained me. 'You would have the rainbow dress in a single shade, and all the roses be white.' And we ran, ribbons trailing down the hallways.

I tear the seal on the envelope. I reach inside. There is no letter. I shake the envelope to confirm its emptiness. There is nothing but the faint scent of primroses and loneliness. I run my finger on the seal, and I find it's been tampered with, opened and re-sealed. Disappointment flushes me, then alters to anger. Who would steal my sister's letter? And I see Lady Mountberry with triumph in her fingers as they work at the seal, as they tear Emmie's letter and toss it in the fire. Wicked creature. My banishment did not satisfy her – she must utterly sever me from Emmie. The ink is smudging. I shake my tears from the envelope and place it on my meagre table. Emmie cannot yet be married. She must still be at Elderford, for how else would Lady Mountberry get her cruel hands on her correspondence? How I longed to be with her on her wedding day, to gather her a bouquet of wildflowers and dreams, to lower her veil and walk behind her into the hymns. But Emmie is not yet wed. And a song begins in me, half celebration, half memory. I will write her wedding hymns – my gift to her. I reach for my pen.

When I look up from my work, there is noon on my wall, on the hills in my window, and on the woods beyond. I have written the veil and the vow into the hymns with triplets of joy. My hand aches. Caleb – he will be waiting for me. And more music, swirls in B Minor, begins. My hymn. My own wedding hymn. If he asks me.

He is waiting by the grandfather clock. He has not seen me at the top of the stairs. I linger to watch him – there is so much thinking in the way he stands, in the crease between his eyebrows. His shoulders, his shadow, his hand pushing through his dark hair – why are they so grave? A gnawing at my heart. Perhaps he will not ask me? Perhaps he wants no other wife but her? There's fleeing in my ankles. I will run. I will pack my meagre possessions and leave. Though I know not where I will go.

"Charlotte," he calls me. Midnight has passed from his features and now there is only dawn. Dawn golden and promising. I descend, forcing myself not to gallop down the stairs for I know I will end in a heap at his feet. The banister steadies me. I keep my steps calm. The hall echoes about me, and though it is still festooned with shadows, they are no longer dour. I am certain they share my glee. And then I am in front of him, and I am all marvel and hush at the amber flecks in his brown eyes. "You had me afeared you weren't coming. If you leave, I will send all the horses in the country on your trail." He takes my hands in his. "Never leave me, Charlotte." And the need in his voice thrills me. And then he clasps me so tightly against his chest that his heartbeat is fast in my ear. "Perhaps I had better hold you forevermore so that you cannot escape," he laughs. Then he releases me. I can inhale once more.

"I could flee while you sleep," I tease.

"I had not considered that catastrophe. Then I renounce sleep. From this moment, I shall always be awake." He strokes my hair. "Come to the woods, Charlotte." And I say nothing but can only nod.

He wraps my cloak about my shoulders and the touch of his fingers on my neck still lingers as we walk the corridors, as we step outside. The door closes behind us. When I step back through the doorway, we will be... we will be... I dare not say the word even to myself. Spring is on the hills. The White Horse is March bright. The sheep bumble cloud-like on the slopes. Though the breeze is cool it smells of green and growing. I breathe the day in down to my toes.

"Come to the woods, Charlotte." He entwines his fingers in mine. We walk in the sparrow song. The birds are with us: robins and fieldfares and wrens. Rabbits are white tails flashing into hedgerows. The wind nudges my bonnet. And I see Ma, a bullfinch tame upon her shoulder. 'This is Jacob and he's teaching me the words of the birds,' she'd said and whistled like rubies. My heart tugs. But my hand is small in his and he is all purpose and onwards. And when we have trekked far enough for Moorvale to be small behind us, I look back. The grim walls ignore the spring sunshine. The dark windows are closed eyes. Yet, I feel a squirrel's inch of affection for the gloomy mansion. Then I see a face. A white face at a high window. A window in the forbidden wing. Her hair is black. Her eyes burning. I gasp. My knees falter. But when I blink, she is gone. "Charlotte, is something the matter?" His hand is on my elbow, grounding me. I shake my head. It was my fancy. It was my guilt. From here, the house is small enough to fit in a wheelbarrow and be pushed about the fields, so how could I even be certain of what I saw? And the windows are black and reflection full. They hold nothing but the hills. What a dilly head I am! I turn away from Moorvale, and I let him lead me.

The woods are tender with blossom. The wind is ivory and pink falling over our path. And the sunlight is wide and welcoming.

All is rustle and song and his hand in mine. The shadows move dolcissimo over us. A deer treads between the graceful trees. We pause and watch and quietness billows in us and peace sighs from the deep of the woods. How the deer goes softly into the green. And I feel I'm a child again, following a fawn in the edges of the south field where the day meets the dark. I find myself brushing away a tear. His glance on me. I pretend I am adjusting my bonnet. And before I can protest, he unties the ribbon and snatches my bonnet aloft.

"Your hair. I have longed to see you with it loose about your shoulders. Will you indulge me and let it down?"

"I do not believe that loose hair would be correct for a governess. And it is in my contract to be properly attired at all times." I smile, but I reach for the combs in my hair, and shake it until it is golden down my back.

"The colour. It is fortunate that you did not live in Ancient Greece or Jason and his Argonauts would have quested for you."

"Are you likening me to a sheep?"

"A golden sheep. It's the highest compliment. No one has ever been so flattered."

"And will we dine on grass tonight?"

"Only the finest grass." We laugh so loudly it muffles the woods. He bends, picks a purple crocus, and tucks it in my hair. "You are beautiful, Charlotte." A gust nudges the trees, and we are standing in a shower of white blossom. I lift my hands in it, catch the pale blooms, then let them fall. Blossom is all over him.

"You cannot return to Moorvale with blossom in your hair. Drellop will jump to conclusions and think it confetti and the next moment all the servants will be gossiping that you've had a secret wedding," I laugh. But he is all longing and gazing.

"You are insufficiently adorned for a wedding." He plucks primroses and pushes them into my hair, his hands as gentle as the sky between the branches, as the clouds wisping above. The breeze feels like forever. His touch aches through me. I stand stone still, I will myself into marble, so not to shed my crown of flowers. How I wish to wear it always. How I wish to be here always. Always in the woods swaying with spring, in the lullaby of rustling. Cool petals moult onto my face and he lifts them so tenderly it hurts me. Then he takes a step backwards, his eyes glistening. "Much better. Now you could be

Tatiana, Queen of the Fairies on her wedding day. She's gliding through the woods to meet her groom, though it would be a better scene by moonlight. Even the stars would envy her looks." I am half daunted, half embarrassed by the hunger in his gaze. I am no queen, fairy or otherwise. My habitat is the mundane and the dreary: a classroom, a corridor. I look down – there are no silver slippers on my feet, only my dust-dull governess boots.

"And who would Tatiana wed? Some raven king cursed to walk as a man by day, and hunt on the wing by night?"

"I would fight such a creature for you."

"You are such a creature," I smile.

"Then it is inevitable. I shall have the banns read." But he does not laugh, he reaches into the inner pocket of his jacket, and produces a green velvet box. "Will you be my wife, Charlotte?" I am shock and hush and weeping and primroses falling from my crown as I nod. The woods whirl with me, and the wind is a waltz in the trees, in the blossom falling like confetti. He is laughing and clutching me, and my crown is tumbling is pressed between us. Primroses crush against his chest. I am arpeggios skipping into octaves. The very air is appassionato. His hands are in my hair. I hear myself laughing, though my face is wet. "Wait. The ring. Hold out your hand." And I do. And I close my eyes. I feel the smooth metal glide. I feel the ring cool on my finger. "It's been in my family for generations. I cannot even tell you how old it is. Perhaps you'll recognise it from all those portraits in the halls throughout Moorvale. I could make a claim that it is as old as those hills, as old that wretched White Horse," he laughs. I open my eyes. I gasp. I falter. My hand flutters, but he holds my wrist firm. An opal in silver. Fire in a white stone. The ring from my dreams.

Chapter Fifteen

Lady Selwyn. I wear her ring. I will wear her name. I hold her husband's hand. I see her house, beyond the fields, small and dark. And as we troop, it widens, it grows. Will Moorvale let me in? Will it let me walk in those halls as his bride? Will it let my portrait hang on its wall? I cannot see myself among those venerable dames, those ladies with history on their brows and nobility in their resting hands. Swaddle me in pearls and velvet and I will still be poppy fields and strawberry jam. I am the forever cuckoo, the lost and found. Am I found now or am I lost? Am I walking home? I have been peasant then lady then governess, and I will be a lady once more. Though there's worry in my steps. I slow down. I do not want to arrive.

"If only we could live our whole lives in the woods," I say, as our hands swing together. Crows circle.

"If you wish, I shall have silver birches planted inside Moorvale's corridors, and yew trees in the ballroom. We shall have our own woods without rain."

"I should think the clouds would follow Drellop inside," I smile.

"Then we will be chased out by hailstorms and forced to seek employment in the circus." We laugh.

Drellop greets us at the door. A Drellop in C Major. She looks at me with thankfulness in her eyes. I am surprised she doesn't begrudge me. For she had such pride in Lady Selwyn, in Faith, in her midnight beauty and her wolf heart. How she disdained noon and sparrow me. Yet here we are, and she has placed a glad hand on my arm.

"Charlotte has agreed to marry me," he says, his voice celebration.

"I can tell. You have my deepest congratulations, Lord Sclwyn, Miss Chant." Her smile is so broad, all I see is teeth. There is a dazzle in the air. Then he is barrelling along, so swift my steps are triplets to his strides. He is holding my hand so hard it hurts. And when we reach the great hallway, he stops. In the chorus of shadows, the Lady Selwyns peer slyly through the gloom. What is the collective noun for such creatures? A celestial of Lady Selwyns? An omen?

What must they think of me now that I wear their ring? Fire in a white stone. It burns on their hands. I haven't got a snail's sense. There was no premonition in my dream. I had seen the ring countless times. I had marched past it, taught beside it.

"Are you waiting for introductions, Charlotte?" he laughs. He points to a portrait. She has auburn ringlets, a cherub chin, and the smile of someone who knows they are the beauty of their era. "Meet my great grandmother, Bathsheba. She had a scathing wit and an appetite for evensong. Her most treasured companion was her piebald mare, Pippin." He smiles.

"Pleased to meet you, Lady Selwyn." I curtsy. He nods at the next painting.

"And this is her daughter, my grandmother. I named Prudence in her honour." Though she has ebony tresses, there is weasel about her smile and in the slope of her eyebrows.

"There is a resemblance," I nod. Then feeling guilty, I add, "She must have been a wonderful grandmother. There is such cleverness in her face. Did she read adventure books to you as you fell asleep?" But he does not look tenderly upon me. The air has talons.

Lines between his eyebrows. How have I misspoken? Was she a grandmother of vinegar and brambles? Did she smack him if he rested a muddy hand on her skirts?

"I never knew her. She died before I was born."

"Caleb, I'm so sorry." I grip his sleeve, but he does not envelope me. "She was young?"

"Yes." His face is a closed kingdom. I cannot find a path to him. I touch his hand, but his fingers are limp. A melody hints though the hallway, a secret in C Minor. There is the feeling of locked doors and hidden passageways. "Did you know your great grandmother? I can picture her with silver hair, still riding a piebald mare. I have known elderly ladies with tiger hearts. I have been afeared of them." I laugh to lighten his solemnity. And then I remember Mr. Wellack telling me of Faith's fate. His ruddy face, his spaniel smell – 'the same thing happened to all the Lady Selwyns. Frost is creeping in me. Did they all suffer so? And I wear their ring and I will wear their name. My heart is a wren. I am chilling to my bones, to my breath. And he is watching me with falcon in his gaze. Then he laughs.

"I called her Sheba, for she wouldn't allow any 'great grandmama' nonsense. I certainly never sat on her knee while she sang me a lullaby. Though she had a small fondness for me, I was no horse." He smiles and puts his arm around my shoulders. "She was frail and elderly when she passed, her body could not compete with her spirit. Her last comment to me was about my inferior riding skills." Suddenly, he kisses my forehead. It sparkles through me. "Enough of this. There will be a better time for choosing the perfect position for your portrait. There's a celebration this evening for us, our engagement. I had intended it to be a surprise, but I can see you will dawdle all day on this very spot. And I have matters to attend to first."

"A celebration? Oh Caleb, there is no need. I am content."

"Well, I'm not content. I want to proclaim it from the rooftops, and if you don't allow me this one evening to do so, you will likely find me many an afternoon shouting from the chimneys. I would make quite the nuisance of myself." He smiles but there's impatience in the way his hands thrust into his jacket pockets. And though I do not want a celebration with strangers, I smile. His gaze widens. "You've saved me, Charlotte." There's a tremor in his voice. Then he strides off, and I hear him asking for his horse.

And I am alone with the Lady Selwyns. I curtsy once more. And I start towards the stairs, towards my little room with its narrow bed and worn rug, but Mr. Wellack's words echo in me. I turn and, in the window, I see Caleb riding out on his black horse, a fast shape in the spring sun. How proud Bathsheba would have been to see him. But only if… Why do I doubt him? Why would he lie about his great grandmother? Yet, I find myself winding through the corridors, past rooms, stepping into the green at the back of Moorvale. There is only a brisk walk to the church, to the graveyard. And why should I linger inside as a companion to shadows when the spring sunshine is fanfares and bunting and scones piled with clotted cream? I walk arm in arm with March along the daffodil path. The breeze is in my bonnet. I nod a greeting at the village folk I pass, and I shake off their bramble stares. The clouds wisp to nothing.

And then I'm at the church. There are rooks and crows bickering on the roof. Or are they warning me? Does this rook with a bald patch on its left wing know the Lady Selwyns' fates? Did the crow that swooped onto the oak above me recognise my ring? Has that blackbird peering out from behind the moss crumbled gravestones…? I am spooking myself. What is there to be afeared of in this hallowed place? The very wind has taken off its cloak to tiptoe through the shadows. There is peace in the ancient stones and worn names. I read years that are too long ago for me to imagine, years from the youth of the White Horse. And I feel awed and small. A robin hops from the holly and goes on its dappled way. Shadows stroke me. My breathing feels like sleep. I lean against the wall of the church. The stone is cool through my cloak, through my dress. I will be wed here. I will become Lady Selwyn here. The bells will proclaim me. And the master will be my home. And I will be his wife. The raven's bride. My heart is rabbit quick, and I am dizzying. Emmie, dearest sister, you were wrong to warn me away from appassionato heroes. For though he is the wolf hour and mid-winter's bite, he is also the tender dawn. We were in the woods - he made me a crown of flowers – he says I have saved him.

I will cease this daft quest. I step from the wall, picking my way carefully between the gravestones, and I read the names as I pass:

Mary Seabourne 1673–1745. Joseph Wellbeloved 1587–1629. Elspeth Binding 1699–1753. And then my gaze is pulled to the far side of the graveyard, under the yew trees to the tomb. How old it looks – as if it were here before the church – as if it grew up from the ground with the hills – as if they shared an infancy. And though it is adorned only in holly and moss, it hints at status and standing. It is the resting place for grand folk. Lords and Ladies. The blackbirds do not gather there, nor the beetles, and there is no rustle of squirrels in the branches above. The sunshine drips slowly through the yews. My breath is catching. And I hear a sadness in G Minor, a gloaming of a tune. It rises from the ground and hangs damp in the air. Whose sorrow is this? It takes my sleeve and leads me between the graves. I do not mean to go to the tomb. I do not mean to run my hand on the time-worn stone, on the rough lichen, on the damp moss. I do not mean to trace the names with my fingers. Selwyn. Selwyn. Selwyn. And there she is, Lady Bathsheba Selwyn 1697–1722. Music roars. He lied. The other names, other dates fall into me. The Lady Selwyns died young. All of them. I see Faith, and I see the space beneath her for my name. And when will they carve the name of Lady Charlotte Selwyn? When will I lie with the others? I wear their ring, I will wear their name, I will share, I will share… The collective noun for Lady Selwyns must be a tomb.

Chapter Sixteen

I am shaking to my footprint. Though I have been hours from the church, from the graveyard, from the tomb. The Lady Selwyns' tomb. I do not know how I found my way to Moorvale when all I saw was green blurred through my tears. But I do know there are rose thorn tears on my skirts, and bramble grazes on my hands. And there is dirt on the hem from the path between the graves. I sit on my narrow bed with my knees pulled up to my chin. I hug my legs. There is so much coldness in me.

    A knock on my door. I unfold from my bed and open it with a trembling hand. It is him. There is joy in how he holds his outstretched arms, in the curl of his lips. And he is handsome, so handsome. But his beauty is made of iron and omens. And as his hands runs down my back, I chill deeper. But I lean into him. And then his hands are in my hair and he cups my chin and he leans down and his lips are on my lips. There's falling in my feet in my ankles in my knees. And his hands are strong on my waist, holding me up. And I am half weakness, half wingbeats. Music riots. Then he stops, smooths my hair off my forehead.

"Perhaps it's not entirely correct since we are not yet wed, but how could I resist my Tatiana?" There is so much wolf in his gaze. I am bitten by it. And something answers in me, and I am pressing against him, and his heartbeat is in me.

"I am the queen of lessons and inkwells, nothing more," I say.

"Charlotte, you do not see yourself as you are. You're a gift. You have saved me. The dark world I lived in has gone. You have lit a thousand candles. You have lit a thousand lamps." His voice catches. "You have changed everything, Charlotte." He moves back from me into the corridor. I see him signal to someone out of sight. Then Mary appears, her eyes narrow. Her sullen arms thrust a golden gown towards me. I take it, am weighted down by it, am struggling not to let it drop. How the embroidery shines.

"What is this?"

"All your learning and you can't recognise a dress, Miss?"

"That's enough, Mary." He steps forward, scoops up the dress and then holds it against me. I look down at pale gold silk embroidered with sunflowers. "When I first saw you, you seemed like a sunflower. And you were – a sunflower that grew in a winter garden."

"It's better than a golden sheep," I smile.

Dusk comes and Mary's bitter fingers attach my stays, tighten my bodice. There is silence but for the rustle of the silk. A luxurious rustling that I wish to sink into and sleep, but there are guests waiting for me. There are folk downstairs who disdained me as Miss Chant yet will now accept me as Lady Selwyn. The wren in my chest beats its wings.

"Your golden shoes, Miss Chant." I hear a thud. Mary has dropped them on the rug. I slip my stocking feet into them, and when I look up, she has gone. I am glad. How she shrank the air. How she dulled the embroidery. I lift my skirts, see the sunflowers glimmer. This dress is a celebration. I spin to see the skirts fly out, and though I have no partner, no sister's hand in mine, I dance a reel about my little room. My steps are light and my shoes gleam. I close my eyes and feel the ballrooms of yesterday: the symphonies of candles, the music that linked our arms, and Emmie's laugh softer than butterflies. I bump into my table. It clatters. I open my eyes, rub my sore leg, and try to study myself in my grey mirror. But it is too small. And I can only glimpse myself in pieces: a square of bodice, a sleeve tapering, a slow shine of hair. Do I look the lady? Would Lady Mountberry still see me as that grime-faced straggletag? But I cannot see myself and so out into the corridor I go. I hold up my skirts. My arms ache with the weight of luxury. And past the silk rustle, I hear muffled triumph – the guests are laughing are drinking are feasting. No ball awaits, no delicate joy, only ruckus and song and country leers. Well, I can holler a folksong bawdy and sad. I will best them all. I turn the corner. There's a golden girl in the gloom. I see her. Her hair buttercups, her dress summer. She is gliding towards me. We meet at the mirror. We curtsy. Can I really be her? Is this how he sees me? Am I someone else now I am his? For I am as changed as the maiden who became the raven king's winged bride. And then suddenly, the raven is behind the golden girl, is gathering her in his black wings.

"Well, Charlotte, does the dress have your approval?" He makes eye contact with me in the mirror.

"I have never felt so much like a legendary sheep," I smile. And the golden girl smiles, too. He lifts my hand to his lips.

"Then it is a great success, my Tatiana."

"Tatiana never had such a dress."

"Maybe she was never so loved. Come, I want them all to see you." And he is marching me in lamplight and shadows towards the carousing. But I hardly feel his hand pulling my arm, or myself striding to keep up. I hardly notice the stairway carrying us down, the archway passing over us, the candles swarming, the great table laden, the folk falling silent, their eyes like beetles over me. For he said... he said...Tatiana was never so loved. Never so loved as I.

"My wife to be – Charlotte. The next Lady Selwyn." There are trumpets in his voice. How proud he is. He doesn't see those two elderly ladies in widow black shaking their heads. He doesn't hear that whisper passing round the table, or the laughter that bursts from behind hands. He doesn't notice that only one guest applauds me. A young woman with fieldmouse eyes. Her limping claps stop. Silence fidgets. The air sweats with the smells of roast piglets and cloves. Hunger nudges me, though I would rather graze on the hills with the sheep. "Come." And I go. His hand leads me to an empty chair at one end of the table where I will be a whole thirty-villagers distance from him. A distance of thorns and sneers, of the wildflower maidens who preen at him, of the ruddy-faced fellows leering. He holds out the chair. I gather my dress and I lower myself. My skirts are wide about me. The silk the gold the rustle the embroidery. How vulnerable the gown is to a greasy chicken bone or splash of ale. I fear its ruin. Lady Mountberry said I doomed fine clothes and I ought to wear full battle armour at the dinner table. I must sup only on water and sour looks.

Caleb's warm hand smooths my hair. It fizzes through me. He smiles and my longing to be alone with him is piercing and sweet. I watch him walk to the head of the table. He lifts a glass. And all the folk lift theirs.

"To Charlotte, my wife to be. I ask you to welcome her, though I know there are those of you who think I am acting in haste, that my judgement is faulty, that I'm making a fool of myself." He pauses. The air is tight. He could be a distance of thirty hundred villagers, or thirty thousand. He turns to a sparrowhawk of a woman. "Mrs. Treewell, I know you've deemed me a silly old fool."

"And not for the first time," she says. Laughter billows. The air eases.

"But Charlotte has delivered me. I did not believe I could be saved." His voice trembles. He holds his glass high, swigs, and then slams it on the table.

So, they feast. And I am forgotten among the crackling meats and sweltering potatoes. And I am glad. I sip water, so's not to imperil my golden dress. And I bathe in the sounds of merriment, until I am half asleep. A man with a wind-burned face starts to sing. All goes quiet.

> *I met a maiden fair and cold*
> *Her face was young, her voice was old.*
> *She took my hand and took my soul*
> *And we walked on the knoll*
>
> *Go softly with me, she said*
> *The beast of Koyn rests his head*
> *If he should wake before I am free*
> *He will devour me*

The beast of Koyn. I startle. Prudence's story. Faith's book. The air feels like water, water soaking my dress, water pulling me downwards. And his song is water too, with clutching weeds and icy currents. I push myself from the table, heave my skirts from the chair, and I go. There are eyes harsh on my back, but then I am out of sight and up the stairs. Faith's rooms. Will they still be hers when I'm the Lady Selwyn? There cannot be any harm in reading her book. I must find it, must read it. And still, he sings in the distance. His song is cold in me and cold in the corridors, though it goes small and vanishes. And then I am at a door. I expect it to be locked, but the handle turns, the hinges creak. I take a lamp, and I enter. The dark smells of violets. Tables and walls and corners and doorways come to the light then retreat. I pass them. My skirts rustle on the floorboards and rugs. And still my dress shines softly. It is my companion. Shame flares in me. Lady Selwyn – I have her ring. And I will have her name and her husband and her home. Moorvale will be mine. These rooms will not be hers. This very gloom that envelopes them will belong to me. Shame and guilt mingle. I have trespassed at her tomb, and I have run my fingers on her name. When I was in her husband's arms, she was in her grave. My conscience slows me, but as I stop to retreat to return to the feast, I see a glow. A glow soft and winding. There is another light. There must be another lamp. So, I follow round the corners through the rooms. A doorway shines and I step into the light. And there she is – the Lady Selwyn seated on her bed, her black hair hanging about her shoulders, her eyes low, her nightdress white. I dare not breathe as she turns the pages of her book and softly reads. Does she know she is dead? Does she know she's a ghost? Yet, how like life she is – the sway of her hair, the blush of her lips, the contentment on her brow. And she is beautiful. So much more beautiful than her portrait. I am washed with envy. A sigh escapes me. She glances up. Despair in her eyes. She raises from her bed, her exquisite face contorting, her black hair flowing. Fear rises in me. I have trespassed. I step backwards, my skirts bump.

"What are you doing here?" Her words are whispers, claws. My voice is lodged in me. I cannot answer. The lamp makes shadows on her. Shadows stretch from her across the floor. The light does not fall through her. She is solid. Solid – the arm that reaches for me – the hand that grips me. I scream.

Chapter Seventeen

"Why are you here?" Her white face is over me, and her hands are hurting me, and I cannot pull away from her. And I hear screaming, screaming coming from me. I try to push her, try to pull her hands from my arms. She scratches me. She scratches me. And then him – him dragging her off me, him restraining her in a corner of the room, him calling to me. My name. My name. I am sinking. All is circles about me. More hands on me. But kind hands – helping me to a chair. I collapse into the seat. And I look up at Drellop.

"You have had a terrible shock, Miss Chant," she says. I hear my teeth chattering. In the corner of the room, he is holding her – the ghost, but not ghost, Lady Selwyn. And she is writhing against his arms, battling to be free. Her hands are talons. How she wants to dig her nails into me. She is violence. I look at the scratches on my hands. I am bleeding. Drellop is kneeling is lifting a handkerchief to my hands is dabbing the blood. It stings. "Faith is ill. You can see for yourself, Miss Chant. She is mad." Drellop produces a vial from her pocket, pours it into a glass, and tops it up with water from a jug. The sounds Lady Selwyn is making chill me, churn me. I do not want to look at her, but I must, I must. Her black hair straggles, her beautiful face is – eyes, teeth, tongue, rage. Rage distorts her. Drellop holds out the glass to her, but she clamps her mouth shut, writhing away from it when it is pressed to her lips. So Drellop pinches the lady's nose. She cannot breathe. She opens her mouth. Drellop grips her chin, pours the liquid in, and hold her mouth shut so she cannot spit it out. The lady's eyes are black fury as she swallows. And still she twists in his arms. Those arms that were wings about me. Those arms that lifted Prudence from the snow. I am shaking and I am still shaking as the lady softens and then goes limp. He lays her on her bed. Drellop covers her with a quilt.

"Charlotte, I couldn't bring myself to tell you. I couldn't let her go to an asylum. It seemed the only way to keep her here. But I had long since fallen out of love with her, though I was ashamed to admit it. And she became a danger to Prudence. It was the only way." He turns to me, his face pleading.

"I saw her tomb. I saw her name." My words shudder. And then he is kneeling by me, his hands clutching mine. He sees the scratches and the blood and lifts my poor hands to his lips. And I am crying.

"You understand, don't you, Charlotte? I couldn't have her rot in an asylum. She would die in such a place. And I would be her murderer."

"I saw her name on the tomb."

"We had to. We had to make everyone believe she was dead." I look past him to Drellop smoothing the tangled hair from the lady's face. There is peace in her countenance, but it is a false peace poured from a vial and forced down her throat.

"And Prudence, does she…"

"I lied to her. She had to believe it."

"You told your daughter her mother was dead." I wrench my hands out of his grasp. I am sobbing so hard it hurts. The poor motherless, but not motherless, girl.

"You think me cruel. You do not know how I have been hollowed out by guilt. You think this was an easy decision? I had my daughter's welfare to think of – better a grieving daughter than a dead one." His head is in his hands.

"She wouldn't hurt her daughter. I don't believe it."

"She already had." He lifts his head. There is so much woundedness in his eyes. "She risked Prudence's life. It was only a matter of time before… You remember I told you my own mother very nearly killed me?"

"Yes," I nod, though I fold my arms about myself.

"I'm not a cruel man, Charlotte. I hope someday you will realise that I only did what I had to do."

"Someday?"

"You no longer want to be my wife." There are tears in his eyes, running down his cheeks.

"You. Have. A. Wife."

"But I want you to be my wife. I need you." His arms clutch at me pull me down from the chair clasp me to him on the floor. "I need you, Charlotte." I am pressed against his chest. My skirts crumple. My heart is ice. Does his wife see how he grips me? Does she hear how he pleads? I wriggle out of his clutches, struggle to my feet, smooth my dress. There is no sign of hearing or seeing in the lady's face. Relief, then shame. I was in his arms, and she was… I wear her ring. I wrench it off and hold it out to him.

"It's her ring. Give it back to her. She's the Lady Selwyn, not me."

"Charlotte, please."

"Miss Chant." I drop the ring, but he doesn't catch it. It rolls on the rug. The lamplight finds it and goes into the opal and gleams fire. A fire that burns me. How weary I am. How I want to fall and not get up. "Give her back her ring," I say. But he doesn't move, his face is wet, his eyes begging. "How could you propose to me?"

"Charlotte, please." He clutches at my skirts. He wraps his arms round my legs. I cannot move. I cease trying. His arms are lead round me. I feel them shaking with his sobs. And still the Lady Selwyn lies in her false grace. And still Drellop smooths her hair with a tender hand.

"You told me I lit a thousand candles." My voice is a wilted thing.

"You have. Charlotte, you cannot fathom how dark my world was before you. Faith's family hid her madness well, well enough for me to marry her. And I thought I loved her – there was so much life in her – she overwhelmed me. But we had not been wed long before she attacked me."

"She attacked you?" He releases his arms, removes his frock coat, and rolls up his right sleeve. Scars. I gasp. I find myself tracing the raised skin on his wrist. And still the touch of his skin fizzes through me, though I am pity and horror. How could such violence dwell in such a fair form? How wrong I have been to envy her ink and moonlight beauty.

"I am covered in them." And there is shame in how he hangs his head, in his arms limp at his sides. A shame I want to lift him from as from a torrid sea. He is innocent. He is wronged. "You see she had a hatred of me. A violent hatred. I had our marriage annulled, but she was with child and Prudence …"

"Annulled? She isn't your wife?" Hope pierces me.

"Faith is not my wife."

"Is that true?" I look to Drellop. And though there's sorrow in her thin lips, in her hands rearranging the lady's blankets, she nods.

"It was not widely known. They have not been husband and wife for years though they have seemed it. The Lord and Lady Selwyn. They had the appearance of being well matched. But who outside these walls could have guessed?" She shakes her head.

"Did she attack you also?" I can hardly bring myself to ask. Drellop nods.

"But you cannot think badly of her, it was not her intention. We manage her the best we can." With fluttering hands, she lowers herself into the chair by the bed. There is so much weariness in the air.

"She has had the finest doctors, but her condition has only worsened," he says. I find my fingers are entwined in his. And I do not pull away. My gaze falls on the ring, on the sad fire in the opal. "Do you forgive me, Charlotte?" But his face is turned away from me. There's a silence that feels like a confession. But the ice has gone from my heart, gone from my veins. I lift his wrist and kiss his scar. And I am all melt as his eyes meet mine, as he traces the tears on my cheeks.

"Yes, I forgive you. You weren't to blame. Her family, they…"

"They did what they thought was best. I bare them no grudge, not now. They knew I would look after their daughter, and I have tried. I have tried." We look at her – the Lady Selwyn. There is no fury in her countenance now. No hatred to mar her beauty. I am filled with pity, overflowing. How her life has been blighted. How much she has lost.

"You don't love her? But she is so beautiful." And now I have no envy, I can allow myself awe and wonder. For never did anyone have such a face. And yet there is no one to see her but her jailers. There was no ghost haunting me, there was only her in the mist and the mirror.

"I thought I loved her once. But it was as like my feelings for you as that lamp is to the sun. You brought me a happiness I couldn't have imagined. I will live on its memory."

"Its memory? Have you given up on me so easily?"

"Is there any hope, Charlotte?"

"Yes," I whisper.

Chapter Eighteen

I dream of a white lady. And a hand cold on mine. A face turning ghostly to me. And a voice in my ear. And we are with the sky. The strange stars are lighting. I taste the night. And the horse is under our feet. Heartbeats, hoofbeats in the ground. Going through me. And she talks, but her words are shapes I cannot catch. And they crowd us – the faces of horn and fang and tongue. They laugh at us. The white lady sings. And there is a being behind us. I feel it rise. I feel its breath.

Then I wake, and the dawn chorus lifts me and there is no fear in the sunshine puddling on my floor, in spring pouring in my window. These days are fresh and dazzling. April has washed the world clean. We do not walk as the wounded. We walk as the healed. And even the rain that falls upon us is all hope and newness. My scratches are gone. And my ring is on my finger. The fire in the opal. And I write for him. I write so much I could write all the inkwells dry. Arias and sonatas, trios, and suites. For him. For him. I do not write down the White Lady's song. I leave it on the hill in my dream, on the chalk horse. But still it follows me: through the corridors of Moorvale, in the fields where we wander arm in arm, in the woods where he holds me. And how curious the melody – half warning, half secrets. It moves from mist to leaping to sorrow and to the sun – the sun setting in the north. But I do not let it tarnish these days. For there are no shadows now. And when he goes to her rooms, it is my sympathy not my envy he carries with him.

Spring glides. The blackbird's beak turns orange. The bluebells are coming. We will be wed on May's eve, though I will not have my sister by my side. I have written and written, but no envelope arrives. And I know Lady Mountberry has torn my wedding invitation to bitter pieces. Does she regret sending me away now that I am to be a lady? Does she pace the south field in fury, mud deepening her hem? Does she sit sullen in the lengthening April dusks? There is both too much April and too little – the oaks are sweet with pale leaves, the hills jumble with lambs, the larks are nesting. And all is slow and delicious. But still, I want to hurry to the last day – our wedding day. When May comes, I will be his wife. Charlotte Selwyn. Lady Charlotte Selwyn. See what has become of Lottie Lion, the straggletag whose hair was flaxen under the grime! And what of my Ma with her

The White Horse

Berkshire burr and dancing walk – would it please her to be mother of a lady? But she cared nothing for titles: her palace was the poppy meadows, her kingdom where the willow wind blows.

How the days sweep by. How can they be so slow, yet so swift? So winding, yet so steady? They have scooped me up and carried me through the flowers and the shadows, the morns and the twilights, and they have set me down here. Here where everything is tomorrow. Tomorrow we will make our vows. Tomorrow the bells will proclaim us wed. And tomorrow we will tell Prudence her mother lives. He protested, but I put my foot down. For I can be as stubborn as a lion with a bellyache and a sore paw, and I will not continue in this cruel play. Mother and daughter must be reunited. How hard it has been not to take the poor motherless but not motherless girl by her hand and lead her to Faith. From my window I can see Prudence meandering on the path. There is so much loneliness in her step, in the hunch of her shoulders. Yet, if she knew – for her father is attending her mother now in the forbidden rooms.

I do not mean to run out into the pale afternoon. I do not mean to call Prudence from her wool-gathering. Yet, I have taken her hand

and am steering her away from the green winds, into Moorvale's gloom. I shut the door on April.

"There's something – I can't explain – you will have to..." I exasperate myself. I put my arm round her thin shoulders and march her through the halls.

"Where are you taking me, Miss Chant? I have finished my lessons with you. Papa will find me a proper governess," she says, but she keeps up. We are allegro to the bottom of the great stairs, allegretto up the steps, and vivace along the corridors.

"I never told you about my mother, Prudence. I lost her when I was younger than you are. It has always been a hollow in me, no matter who else I loved." Wisps of melody circle me, stinging my eyes, and in them I smell poppy fields. "I would give anything to see my Ma again." And we go faster – we are presto – we are prestissimo. And then we are at a closed door. The door to Faith's rooms.

"I'm not allowed in Mama's rooms. Papa won't let me, not even her library." Her pout is grief and defiance.

"Your father is going to allow you in your mother's rooms tomorrow. Tomorrow!"

"I don't believe you."

"It's true. So, it will hardly matter if we're one day early." I grip the handle. There's joy in the creaking of the door hinges. It swings wide and we are bathed in the scent of violets. I usher Prudence inside, though there's so much fleeing in her face. How curious the forbidden wing is at this hour. The daylight moves as if it is unaccustomed to such a habitat. We turn corners, through archways. And I do not know where to find them. I fling the library door open expecting to see the lady serene with her books, but only novels and tomes greet me. Titles gleam in an arrogant hush.

"Papa doesn't allow me in the library. Why are you doing this, Miss Chant? Have you lost your senses?" There's agitation in how she folds and unfolds her arms. Low laughter wafts through the stillness. The music in me thins to an icicle, chilling me. "I want to leave," she whispers.

"No," I say, and take her elbow and we go where the laughter grows. And the music arches through minor keys weighting my steps. And then we are round a corner and the laughter is beaming from the doorway of Faith's bedroom.

"Don't," Prudence says, and her hand is firm on my sleeve, but I am pulled to the doorway. And I see them. How is she entwined in his arms? How is her dark hair fanning on the pillow? How is he kissing her neck? He is mine and I am his and she is mad. But I see them. I see his closed eyes. I see her parted lips. I am falling. Prudence is holding me up. I jolt into a chair. It bumps the wall. And he sees us – his eyes open horror wide.

"I tried to stop her," Prudence says. She stands over me and there is no shock or happiness in her voice. She is not a girl who has just been reunited with her dead mother. A jagged pain moves in me. And he is buttoning his shirt, pulling on his frock coat. And there is no violence in Faith's laughter, no madness in her smile. I look between them. I see their secret.

"Charlotte, I can explain." He reaches for me. He mustn't touch me. I jump out of the chair. And I am out the room, and I run and violet scent chokes me, and corners hit me, and he calls. My name. It is spiders in his voice. I am running and I hear him behind me – heavy and fast. But the doorway shines, and I am nearly there and then I am out of the forbidden rooms. I slam the door behind me. The key is in the lock, and I turn it, I shut them in. I wrench the key out and toss it down the corridor. It flashes. He will not touch me. He will not lure me with lies or with his hands. The memory of his touch shudders through me. I will not see him. And then the door shakes. I step backwards. "Let me out, Charlotte. I have to talk to you, but I cannot do so through a locked door." And in the pause, I can hear his charming smile and his bashful hand in his dark hair. The door rattles harder. "Charlotte, I need to see you. I need you to understand. Sometimes, I have to pretend that Faith and I are still married. It is the only way to manage her illness. How I wish it wasn't necessary, but..."

"She is not ill," I gasp out. The door shakes.

"Charlotte, I need you. Charlotte." He thumps the door. And I am fleeing again. And I am fury and despair and bafflement. The music in me tilts, surges, and clamours. Furioso. The walls swim about me, the shadows mock me. I hear him hitting the door, bellowing my name. I will not let him see me. I will leave. The air is sore in my chest. I stop to breathe, and I find myself near his study. I am a furnace of anger walking through its doorway. How am I not breathing flames? There is so much burning inside me. I am screaming it out of me. I am heaving books off his shelves. I am tearing out handfuls of pages. My face is wet, but still I burn. His desk. His star charts. The stars are Pa Mountberry's and mine. He does not deserve them. I want to take the stars from him. I want to take the sky from him. I pull out one of the drawers so harshly it falls. Envelopes gush out. I crouch. Emmie's handwriting. My name. These are my letters. The letters that never arrived. I tear one open.

Dearest Sister,

And so I am married! But it was a solemn celebration without you, my Lottie Lion. Confetti and tears. Whatever happened to those two girls who planned to wed pirate brothers and sail the seven seas? Are they still plotting in the south field?

My heart hurts so I can barely read. He kept my sister's letters. He stole them. I heave out the other drawer. It is cramped with the star charts. I will tear them to pieces. I am all claws all talons. I pull one out and unfold it on the desk. My breath narrows. There is no Ursa

Major, no Orion, no Sirius. These are not the stars Pa Mountberry showed me. This is not the night sky. Fear rises in me, chokes me. These are the strange stars from my dreams. These are the stars I saw from the White Horse's eye.

Chapter Nineteen

I run my fingers along the strange stars. And I feel small again and alone – when there was no one, just this sky and me. This sky he knows. This sky he has charted. He has stood on the White Horse's eye, but he has not been afeared, he has carried this sky home. Understanding nudges me, then vanishes. For I am all bafflement. Fear is turning me stone-still. And I am rooting when I know I should be running. And all the music is screaming for me to flee.

So I run. He will not be locked in for long. He will chase me. Where will I go? I rush down the corridors down the hallway, past my little room. I dare not stop for coins or my cloak. Onwards, onwards. He will come. They will come. The raven and his bride. She stuck her nails in me and made me bleed. And he lifted my hands and kissed her scratches. The music in me roars.

I am at the stairs. Drellop looks up at me. She poured a vial and forced it into down the lady's throat. But the raven's bride did not really wilt, did not truly sleep. Drellop and the raven and his bride and his daughter – all lie, all deceive. I am inhaling, exhaling fear. But I must descend with calm steps. Now I must fool her.

"Miss Chant, you look flushed. Are you well?"

"Tomorrow will be my wedding day, Drellop. I cannot help but shake with excitement. See." I hold out my trembling hands. And I laugh as best I can. "I should like a hot drink and a fire in my room."

"I shall have Mary tend to it," she nods. She goes. There is no suspicion in her tread. And I go. I am out the front door. The White Horse faces me. The hills look down on me. The winds are with me – smelling of green and escape. Escape to where? I have no friend here. My face is wet. I run and I run – with the wind stinging my cheeks. I do not look back. I trample my hem in the mud. I stumble. Drellop will have found them, will have let them out. They will come for me. And will they bring the strange stars? 'She comes to those who see the sun setting in the north.' Wellack's words. He warned me. And I felt his warning down to my bones, but still I stayed. I go fast. Wellack. The path is too slow and too winding and I am feet and flight and stumble and flinging myself at the door. I beat my fist. I thump the wood. The door swings open. A lady with a face like a sour pancake. I do not wait for invitation; I push inside and heave the door shut behind me.

"Mr. Wellack, please," I gasp out. I slump against the wall. She is footsteps echoing. I watch her back. And then there's the ruddy-faced man who smells of spaniels and wood.

"The Lady Selwyn to be. And to what do I owe this honour?" But there's concern in how he nods for his maid to take me into the front room. I am put in a chair, and I am all shake – shoulders, knees, breath.

"Should I send for the doctor?" the maid asks.

"No! He was, he was…"

"Now you just take your time, Miss. We won't send for the doctor or anyone else for that matter. Not without your say so."

"I need to leave."

"Well, if you ask me, better to leave than end up a Lady Selwyn going the same way as all the other Lady Selwyns." There's a half joke in his smile but worry in his creased forehead.

"He, he…"

"No need to tell me. Won't take long to get the horses saddled. Elspeth here is going to fetch you a drink, something strong. Now you just sit tight." He winks. Relief is flooding me is tumbling me is rapids in me. I am sobs and thankfulness. He will help me. I will be free. My body is lead with relief. I do not think I have ever been so heavy. Elspeth is by me, pushing a glass in my hand. Whisky tingles my nose.

"Won't be long, Miss," she says. The glass tremors in my grip. I sip and I slump but inside I am hurry, hurry, please hurry. A click. It jolts me. A key in a lock. Am I? Have they? I drop the glass on the floor and it shatters and whisky splashes and I am hurling myself. The handle won't turn. The door won't open. They locked me in. And in the window, I see Elspeth on the path, wind in her dress. She is calling out. She is waving her arms. To whom does she wave? To whom does she call? But I know it is him, I know it is him. Him striding towards her. Him looking towards the house. Him seeing me. My legs go out from under me, and the floor comes up to me. He is coming. The room is round me – it has no hiding in it, no help in it. I scrabble to my feet. I hear footsteps on the path – his voice – his voice. Then the key in the lock. I flee to the far corner of the room, behind a weighty chair.

The door opens and there he is. His gaze is snakes on me. My hands jolt on the chair.

"Charlotte, darling – this is all just a misunderstanding." How did I not see before the viper in his charming smile? I am so flooded with loathing it strengthens me.

"Misunderstanding or not. I require my sister's company, and I shall be leaving this afternoon."

"Our wedding is tomorrow."

"I'm leaving this afternoon." I meet him with a lion stare. My chin is high, but wobbling. He laughs and runs his hand through his hair.

"Anything you need," he nods, and takes benign steps across the room. I am raw with hatred, but I give him a dove smile, and I let him near me. He is handsomeness made with cruelty. He reaches for me. I duck, dart across the room, push Elspeth out my way, then I am in the hall and out the front door. I rush in the green, I breathe it, I pelt, I ache. Footsteps closer and closer – I am wrenched from my running. I am held aloft. Arms like iron haul me up. I am screaming. I am writhing, but he holds me so I cannot get free. And there is no one – no one to help me. The air is bitter.

"Let me go," I gasp out.

"It is an amusing game that you're playing, Charlotte. But I need you. I need you to be my wife. We will be wed tomorrow." I am over his shoulder. I hit his back.

"I will not be your wife," I shout, but he marches onward. And I try to kick and hit and writhe, but still, he holds me tight. And there is no tiring in him – it is as if he carries a doll. "I. Will. Not. Be. Your. Wife." But he ignores me. I cease. I go limp. I cannot get away. I save my fighting. He is going up steps, then a doorway passes over us, and I smell Moorvale – its secrets, its gloom.

"What will you do with her?" It is she who speaks, the raven's bride, the false ghost. I am glad I cannot see her peerless face. "We can't risk her escaping. Put her in the chapel," she says. And we go on, and though I cannot see the lady, I hear her dolce step. Her violet scent sickens me. She is ahead of us up the stairs, down the hall, past my little room. My room where I had dreamed of my wedding day. And then we are passing through another door. I feel space about me

– dark and aged. A door shuts behind us. And he puts me down. My ankles wobble. We stand, the three of us, on a landing, near a carved ceiling, and in the deeps below is the chapel. The only windows are high are narrow – only a stoat could climb to them and crawl through them. He grips my upper arm and forces me down the stairway. She follows us – her violet scent. The chapel grows about us: pews and gilt and an altar. But there is no saint or cross on the altar cloth. There is only the White Horse. Fear slashes through me. Do they worship here – the raven and his bride? To what do they pray? I look up at the ceiling and I see a shining pattern – stars – the stars I saw from the White Horse's eye. The music in me is past warnings, past rescues. How will I get free?

"What do you want with me?" I face them. How horrid their beauty is now – how unnatural her face without a flaw. Revulsion blooms in me.

"I only wish to marry you, Charlotte." He begins a lovestruck look, but it is mockery.

"Yet, you have a wife."

"What have you heard about the Lady Selwyns?" she asks. "Why did you visit our tomb?"

"Wellack told me you all died young. It seems he was incorrect." I smile at her. And she laughs as if we three were childhood friends. I am a fortress of indignation. "Why did you haunt me? If it was so vital that I marry him, why scare me? I could have fled." And I spy a flicker of jealousy in her jewel eyes. "You did not care for it, did you? Do you think it was all pretty speeches and hand holding?" I shake my head at her. How can her white face be paling? He reaches to seize me, to shut me up, but I dart out of his grip. "I could be with his child now. A brother or sister for Prudence."

"Is this true?" She spins to him. But his expression sparks hope in me – for there is a hint of feeling for me. Perhaps he will relent? Perhaps he will let me go?

"She was nothing I expected – her music – I had never heard anything like it before. I had never met anyone like her before."

"That was your wedding night," Faith spits.

"It was not a single night," I taunt her. Her face comes close to mine. There's terror in her beauty. I try not to shake. I clench my fists, dig my nails into my palms.

"I thought I might feel guilt when it devours you. But all I will feel is pleasure." A wolf smile. She calls for Drellop. And then the two women have seized me and Drellop is pressing a glass against my lips. I shake my head, writhe. Faith pinches my nose. I cannot breathe. I cannot breathe. And he won't look at me. I open my mouth, snatch a breath. Faith grips my chin, pours the liquid in, holds my mouth shut. And I am swallowing.

Chapter Twenty

The moon is thin. The stars are still. The White Lady walks on Dragon Hill. The wind is in her pale dress. Her step is light, her hair flowing. She is searching. She is seeking. And in her heart and in her tears is her home. Her home so far away, so long ago. But there is a poison in the ground and there is a creature that sleeps. And then there is a waking.

My name. My name. It is shaking me. A damp cloth cold on my face. I open my eyes. A blur becomes his shape. Him. I shrink from his touch. And all around me is the gloom that reaches to high, narrow windows, and above them, strange stars in a carved ceiling. The chapel is rich with darkness. I do not know if this is night or day. There is so much weakness in me. Memory ignites me – Faith and Drellop pouring liquid down my throat – the heaviness, the sinking. I look down at myself. I am in a chair, and I have been placed in a white dress. My ankles are tied.

"Did you…" I begin.

"Faith changed you into your wedding dress."

"Why are you marrying me?" My voice is groggy.

"It has always been the Lord Selwyn's wife. Always. You saw the tomb. You saw how far back it goes. Yet, my mother thought that she could escape it. It wouldn't devour her, not her, for she was descended from the White Lady. Or so she fancied."

"What happened?"

"She even went so far as to claim the White Lady came to her dreams, showed her how to…" He inhales loudly. "I believed her. And I wore hay and went to the hill. I held my father's hand. And I was proud my mother looked so well. I was not afeared until she stood on the White Horse's eye, until she turned to look at me. Her face – it was as if she saw a monster not her son. I wanted to run. I felt it come. I ran and I ran, and I didn't look back."

"What about the White Lady?"

"There was no White Lady. My mother was gone. And I grew from boyhood knowing my wife would follow her. Can you understand, Charlotte, what it is to grow up knowing you must send your own wife to her death?" He looks imploringly at me. I am not so drugged that I would sympathise with my murderer. I want to scratch his handsome face. My hands are talons – but tied, tied. My wrists are bound tightly to the arms of the chair.

"You needed me to be your spare wife. How funny that you likened me to a sheep when I am your lamb."

"I did not know you when I decided on this solution. I did not know it would be you." And there is both tenderness and sorrow in his voice. But it inflames me. How dare he be contrite when he keeps me prisoner.

"But now you do know me, and yet you will still send me to my death." How I wish I were my nickname – a lion. I would savage him.

"Charlotte, please, if you knew how I have been tormented, you wouldn't look at me so."

"I have no option other than to look at you. Let me go, and I will gladly never look at you again in my life."

"Charlotte, I wish I could let you go. In another life, we may have…" He trails off. Then his hands are touching me, my hair, my face. I repress a shudder, for his touch is wasps now. But if he has an affection for me, maybe… maybe… There's a pinprick of hope. And so I let him lift my chin, I let him place his lips on mine. And I close my eyes in mock ecstasy. How gently he kisses me, as if we were sweethearts in bluebell time. He moves away. He is at the altar. The White Horse is bright on the cloth behind him.

"Let me go, please," I whisper. Footsteps. Footsteps. She is coming. His hands fidget, his shoulders brace. He will let me go. It is in his face. He will. He will. But then he shakes his head.

"I cannot."

"I will look at you when I die. And you will carry it with you all your days." And his eyes shine tears, but still, he does not help me. I am lost. I will never see Emmie again. And she will never know what became of me. She will look for me, and she will never find me. Bitter tears run down my face. Footsteps. Then the scent of violets and cruelty.

"It is tradition to be joyful on your wedding day," she laughs. Her glorious face is all triumph. There's merriment in how she flicks her hair. I fight to stop my tears. How curiously she is dressed – there is hay tied in bundles to her gown. And she is not alone. Another figure. I balk as I recognise him – the vicar. And there is hay on his plain robe.

"Why do you…" I begin.

"It is already May Day," she snaps. "You slumbered through what was intended to be your wedding day, so now we have to hurry. Why do you look at me so? They never wore hay in whatever village you came from?"

"My Ma was Berkshire through and through," I say. But she ignores me as the vicar speaks low into her ear. And then Caleb is crouching and untying me. I do not resist as he lifts me to my feet. I do not pull away when he takes my arm and leads me to the altar. And the White Lady's melody is so loud in me, I wonder how they do not hear it.

The vicar is behind the altar. He raises his left hand. He makes carving motions in the air. I am steel and I am thorns and I am not faltering or shaking. The vicar chants and the words are strange. And she joins and he answers. Their voices swim in me. For the White Lady spoke in a dream and her words had these shapes. I am dizzying.

And I recall her cool hand on my arm. And her eyes – ghostly and kind. There was something of my Ma in the arch of her eyebrows.

Silence. It jolts me.

"Was that all?" I glance at him.

"We are wed." His voice is bleak.

Chapter Twenty-One

A dark door opens. Day comes into the chapel, goes over the carved faces gruesome on the pews, onto the altar cloth with the White Horse, and onto me. The white of my dress smarts my eyes. Then the doorway is passing over me, and I am taken into May. It smells of dew and waking. The wind is birdsong. If only I could lift my arms into the sun falling golden upon me. But his grip on my arm is strong, is leading me, and I am going to the hill. I do not struggle, for I am breathing in my last morning. The starlings swirling, the clouds bumbling, and the lambs gentle among the green. The path is rough under my bare feet. I do not look at my executioner with his vice grip. I do not turn when I smell violets and hear soft steps behind me. I pretend I am alone. But then the others come.

We are a crowd. We are many. We are the village. There is chatter and play and merriment and hay. Hay tied to dresses and smocks. And it feels like festival, not like death. But there is no hay on my dress. My dress trails in the grass, soaks up dew, is cold against my legs. A little girl with flaxen tresses points at me.

"Look, Mama, the White Lady," she giggles.

Up and up and up. I am glad my feet are bare for I can feel the dew between my toes. And I am grateful there is no bonnet to keep the wind from my hair. The sky has joined us. We are above the world. I can see right to its edges. And I breathe in those patchworks of fields. I do not look down the slope. But I feel the shine of chalk in sun. And something cracks in me. Fear rises up, closes over me. My gasps sting. I pull. I scratch. He doesn't let go.

"Charlotte, please," he says. His face, his handsome face. Sorry in his eyes, but not in his hands that hold down my arms. He hurts me. He hurts me. My face is wet. He shakes his head at me.

"Put her on the eye," Faith says. Her face is near mine - her marchpane breath - her jewel eyes. And the folk are behind her – there's so much waiting in them, so much spectacle. Faith and him, seize me, force me. I am nearly falling. The ground slopes away, and down onto the white, the chalk. And then I am on the eye.

Silence takes me and holds me. The sun is rolling fast, fast over the sky, fast down the hill. It is low, it is lower, it is setting in the north. Gold turns to orange turns to red turns to dark. Am I in the dark?

Am I here? I look down to see my hands. I lift them. And the sky is between my fingers. And there are the strange stars. I trace those patterns, and coldness comes from them and goes into me. And it feels old. Silence gleams. Am I alone? I turn to look at him. A scream moves in me – barrels from me. His face, his handsome face – is gone. His features are pulled down and dark and he is monstrous. And her – her jewel eyes are rot and chasm. Her mouth is tongue. And past her – them – the village folk, with their hay and laughter – they are, they are fang and horn and judder and drool. I want to run. I want to run. My feet are rooted. I have no screaming left. I am seeing what the White Horse sees. I am seeing that they are monsters.

There is a beating in the ground. Soft and growing. Growing until it thuds. Thuds through my feet, my ankles. Until I jolt with each beat. Is this my death? The monsters jeer. I look at his face. How like his devil mask it is. How like the devil he is. I am wracked and shaking. My ring – I lift my hand – the opal shines fire. I wear the devil's ring. My fingers can't grasp, can't pull. I cannot take it off. The beating is all through me. And they watch, they watch. There is hunger in their monster eyes. It is coming. It is coming. I brace. I do not fall. I feel it rise. I feel its breath.

Suddenly, in the vale below is a ghost. Her hair is white, her dress whisper. She moves like wind. Her feet so light. Does she soar or does she bound? She is swift. Swift up the hill. Her cool hands are on my wrists. Her voice is soft on my face. And her face – her face. There is something of my mother about her face. And I know. I know who I am. For I have come from her. She takes me in her arms. But still it rises behind me. Still it breathes on me. The White Lady speaks shapes. I catch them and her song comes. And it is all through me and funnelling out of me. My voice is white. The beast lowers to me. There is a sound like jaws like hunger. I feel the wind as the beast turns, and I do not look. I shut my eyes. And the White Lady's arms are round me. And the song still comes. But there are other sounds. The folk. The monsters. Is this terror I hear their death? The hill sways. Horror – their screams – their bones – their silence. I do not know how I keep singing. I shut my eyes harder. I mustn't look. I mustn't look. And still the sounds shudder me. I want to run. The ground is shaking. But the White Lady holds me, keeps me in her song. Her cool arms. The screams go one by one. One by one the beast has them. The monsters. One last voice. One last scream. I know it is him. I know the beast has him. How it curdles me. And then he is silent. Silent. All is silent. But still it moves. It lowers to us. It breathes on us. I brace. But I sing. And then it is lowering and lowering and lowering. And it has gone back into the hill.

I open my eyes. I am stuck in my fear. I do not turn around. I do not know if it is worse to see the monsters, or to see that they are gone. The White Lady lets go of me. Though her face is near mine. And I can see my Ma in her, and I can see myself in her. And I know I came from her. How I wondered who I was. How it hollowed me. Peasant or lady? Lady or peasant? Her ghostly face shines kindness and shines kin. Silence hangs on us. I turn. There is no one. No crowd. No folk. No her. No him. There are scraps of hay, but there are no monsters. There is no beast. Relief puts me on my knees. I am alive. I will live. I sob thankfulness. But when I look up, the White Lady is already down the slope, already swift into the vale. I call to her. I start after her. I step off the eye. Sunlight crashes upon me. The night is gone. The day is sweet with May, in lamb and wind and kestrel and the patchworks to the edges of the world. Sun warms me. I raise my arms into the golden winds. And they are in my hair and my dress. Joy lifts me and runs with me. And I go and go and there is nothing to chase me or to take me down into the hill.

Epilogue

Ten years later.

The gloom still smells of violets, though dust has fallen like sleep, and I leave footprints trailing behind me through the great hall where he toasted me, the corridors where he held me, and into the chapel where he wed me. Light thins through the narrow windows. I tread adagio down the stairs. I move between the pews as if not to disturb prayers. And I place my sheet music on the altar. I will leave it here where no one will find it, no one will play it. The White Lady's song. How it saved me. How it delivered me. Yet, I could never write it out – for if the melody visited me in my dreams or waking, it brought a beating in the ground. The beast. The beast. And so, I plunged myself into other music. And Oricala, dear Oricala, took me away, took me to kingdoms that were symphonies that then carried into all the cities of Europe. For I am toasted far and wide. Charlotte Mountberry. The Mountberry Marvel. But I am still poppy fields and strawberry jam, no matter which duke or prince pursues me. And when they propose, I tell them I am wed to Oricala. How Emmie and I laugh, and I play a dancing tune to the twilight, and through the open windows we hear two girls, and they come running by, their hems trailing summer. Two girls, one dark haired, one golden. And they are not ghosts or memories. My golden girl, Anna. Though she does not know she is mine, and she calls me her lion aunt. I see my Ma in her. One day, we will walk in the poppy fields. They are still waiting for me to come home.

About the Author

Rebecca Harrison comes from Wokingham, Berkshire. The White Horse of Uffington was one of her favourite places growing up, and she has so many memories of family outings: the first glimpse of the chalk figure, the hillside falling away by the road, the steep climb to the top of the hill, dodging sheep muck and biting winds, and then the view right out to forever.

Also Available from Spooky House Press

Deeply Personal by Alexis Macaluso

Boarded Windows, Dead Leaves by Michael Jess Alexander

Her Infernal Name & Other Nightmares by Robert P. Ottone

The Girl in the Floor by Robert P. Ottone (Kindle Vella)

Helicopter Parenting in the Age of Drone Warfare by Patrick Barb

Coming Soon

Her Teeth, Like Waves by Nikki R. Leigh

Residents of Honeysuckle Cottage by Elizabeth Davidson

Into the Gray by Kathleen Palm

The Disappearance of Tom Nero by TJ Price